D1738039

SAVE ME,
JOE LOUIS

SAVE ME,
JOE LOUIS

A Novel

M. T. Kelly

Published in 1998 by Stoddart Publishing Co. Limited
34 Lesmill Road, Toronto, Canada M3B 2T6
180 Varick Street, 9th Floor, New York, NY 10014

Distributed in Canada by General Distribution Services Ltd.
325 Humber College Blvd., Toronto, Canada M9W 7C3
Tel. (416) 213-1919   Fax (416) 213-1917
Email customer.service@ccmailgw.genpub.com

For information about U.S. publication and
distribution of Stoddart Books, contact
180 Varick Street, 9th Floor, New York, NY 10014

02   01   00   99   98   1   2   3   4   5

Canadian Cataloguing in Publication Data

Kelly, M. T. (Milton Terrence), 1947–
Save me, Joe Louis: a novel

ISBN 0-7737-3124-5

I. Title.

PS8571.E4477S28 1998   C813'.54   C98-931472-3
PR9199.3.K44S28 1998

Cover Design: Pekoe Jones
Cover Photograph: Pete Paterson
Text Design: Kinetics Design & Illustration

Printed in Canada

*We gratefully acknowledge the Canada Council for the Arts and the
Ontario Arts Council for their support of our publishing program.*

In the reconstruction of Proto-Indo-European, from which many languages derive, the word "Man" — Old Persian Martiya, Sanskrit marta, Greek Mortos, comes from the root Mer — "to die." And "father," Latin pater, Hittite attas, Luwian tati, Palaic and English papa, Armenian hayr, Old Irish athir, Tocharian pacer, may have connotations with "aid."

IN SEARCH OF THE INDO-EUROPEANS,

J.P. MALLORY

And it came to pass, that, as he was praying in a certain place, when he ceased, one of his disciples said unto him, Lord, teach us to pray, as John also taught his disciples. And he said unto them, When ye pray, say, Father . . .

LUKE 11:1-2

C H A P T E R *1*

THE BOY'S TALENT DIDN'T seem attached to him, to the child he was. "I'll never let him take a beating," Pearce thought.

"What's wrong?"

Automatically, Pearce swept his left out in an arc. Robbie came back with sharp punches.

"Serious shots." Pearce nodded.

"What?" Robbie looked tempted to hit his coach. "You okay?"

"Come on."

The lights were not on over the ring, which kept the back part of the gym dull. No one else around. Monday afternoon, and Robbie should have been in school, but with a mother like his that could not be counted on.

Brightness that came through the plate glass windows at the front of the club never reached this far back. Yet Stuart Ewell Pearce could see a sheen of saliva on the left of Robbie's mouth.

"Take a break," Pearce said.

"What's wrong?" Robbie insisted, his irises wide, a little startled and angry at the interruption.

He's into it, Pearce shook his head, even today he's into it. "Take it easy," he said.

"I like to work the pads."

"I know." The quiet, the darkness, didn't affect how Robbie was going. "But take it easy," Pearce repeated. The lad worked too hard, if that was possible. "Take a break."

Dropping his hands, Robbie turned to the corner.

The split second of a punch, Pearce thought: hours go by. He'd spent so much time at the gym since retiring. The place was funny; weather outside, the seasons themselves, never seemed to get through the glass, not up front with the mirrors and hardwood floor and space, or back by the ring where it was so gloomy with the lights off.

Standing there, sweating a little, unsure of why he'd stopped, feeling he should work out himself, even at his age, Pearce sensed her coming.

It was uncanny, he must have heard something on the stairs. A wind of confusion, Pearce thought, the way she entered a room; you always had to account for her. And yet she didn't speak to them as she walked over to take a seat. Smiling, but not for them, conscious of some kind of role, though she didn't glance their way. Lucy's smile fulfilled an idea she had of what a smile should be, Pearce thought.

So pretty and small, but with something a little awkward about her — the way one stocking wrinkled over an ankle, lipstick too fresh and on her teeth. Pearce could hear her breathe.

Arms at his sides, swinging back and forth, Robbie

stared at his mother. Why did she always have the ability to surprise him? Pearce wondered. You'd think the kid would be used to some of it by now! But then she always seemed to catch *him* off guard as well.

Lucy sat down, crossed her legs. There was a rustle, a strong sigh, and as she put her arm over the back of the chair her stole dropped off one shoulder and hung to the floor.

Maybe we shouldn't say anything this time, Pearce thought. Then, fleetingly, he smiled to himself, comparing the sense of expectation he felt coming off her to a body punch.

"What's up, Mum?" Robbie was ahead of him.

"I don't want him fighting Saturday." She spoke generally, to the room.

Blindsided, Pearce thought, even if I expected it. He consciously exhaled. She's always a workout. Always. "We'll take care of him, Mrs. Blackstone," he said.

"Mum," Robbie said.

"Don't whinge," she spoke to the boy, somehow not really acknowledging him.

She must mean whine, Pearce thought.

"Not against a full-grown man," Lucy added.

"That will never happen." Lord, she had a tiny head, and so blonde.

"That don't mean nothin'," Robbie said.

"It's not simply weight classifications, it's age groups," Pearce explained.

"I just don't want him to get hurt," she said.

Nothing else to do, Pearce thought, coming in here all dressed up in the middle of the day.

"I've got to meet Shiner," she said.

"Ah," Pearce said and wondered if he ever hit her, or the lad. Probably not, in fact he was sure of it. Shiner didn't give them enough attention to do that. And Pearce remembered, to his annoyance — he always remembered it — that time Shiner handed out business cards in the gym. He had to have been lit, but what was extraordinary was the way the boys responded to him, as if Shiner was at a party with a drink in his hand and was somehow powerful. They deferred, wanted this stranger to like them.

A big man in a camel overcoat with red-blond hair and more pink than brick red in his complexion. Clean shaven with skin that looked not chapped but scraped. Freckles on his knuckles.

And Pearce would not forget that business card. After a lifetime of going to stags and being in boxing, and working at the city — there were creeps in his department, all right — Pearce found the card a shock. On one side was his name: WILSON (SHINER) MACLEAN, with three telephone numbers. On the other side was the kind of joke you saw printed on dish towels or engraved under figurines of drunks:

A man has 17 parts that don't work for him
   Ten nails that don't nail
   One bellybutton that doesn't button
   One ass that won't work.

The vulgarity went on to conclude with a challenge to a woman: What are you smiling about? . . . Pearce refused to recite the exact words, but he knew them all right. It might not have been that much different from other jokes about drinking or going to the toilet, but, like those mimeographed obscenities he'd some-times received at the office, the fact the card was printed, that someone had taken the time to have it made formal, gave it more impact. Laughs at this kind of thing were always a little false, with a kind of elusive shame no one seemed to know what to do with. Pearce might have glanced aside, but he had not turned away. Neither had the other men.

"Could you drop me off at the Radio Artists?" Lucy asked.

"Sure," Pearce said, thinking of the atmosphere in the car driving down there in rush hour, creeping along with the windows rolled up as it started to spit rain. "We'll stop what we're doing here."

"Shiner has to entertain," she explained.

"That's fine."

"Clients."

"Yep."

Robbie got out of the ring and walked into the bright foyer of the gym to stand beside his mother. He wasn't sweating, and his skin looked almost grey. Though only twelve years old, he seemed big as he stood over her, big because of the sixteen-ounce gloves and headgear, much bigger than she was. Her dark rustling dress spread around her in a corolla and she looked up, her lips pursed and rubbery as she bit at them.

"You'll get hurt," she said after a pause.

Now Pearce felt obliged to go to her as well, in spite of himself. He ducked between the ropes and jumped heavily down. "Robbie," he said, as if to call him back, at the same time hearing commotion on the stairs.

Wilson "Shiner" Maclean stood in the doorway. Lucy's boyfriend let the room have his smile, which had a lot of grin in it. Even if the smile made him look like he had dentures, it set off his big, square head. Shiner was rugged, a word Lucy used, and had the beginnings of a drinker's nose though without the colour: a little bulbous, indentations starting to flatten it out against his face.

When he saw Shiner, Robbie spun on the ball of his foot and walked away. Beneath his singlet, his shoulders worked; from behind, his body had the shape of a mature flyweight's.

Was she afraid of the guy, did she deliberately make herself smaller? Pearce wasn't sure.

"Hi, Shine," Lucy said.

Not moving, Shiner filled the doorway. Then he took a stride into the room and went over to her, his coat opening as he walked.

"Say hi," Lucy called to Robbie.

The boy ignored her.

Pearce thought of Shiner as Robbie's semi-step-father-in-common-law, and knew the boy was supposed to refer to him as Uncle — Uncle Shine — but the kid wouldn't do it today.

"Perfesser," Shiner said, nodding at Pearce.

He *has* to pronounce it that way deliberately, Pearce thought, or maybe he just is the ignorant bastard he seems. What's next: "If you're so smart why ain't you rich?" But Shiner's manner was too laconic for that.

Stopping behind Lucy's chair, Shiner continued to pay attention to Pearce. She twisted her neck and lifted her face to him. "Hi, hon," she said.

"Everything okay?" Shiner asked Pearce.

"Sure. Why wouldn't it be?"

"Keepin' the boys in line, eh?"

"Nobody's out of line."

Staring past him, Shiner's attention focused on the sign that read: "No profanity: watch your language."

"You know," Shiner said, "I hate that f'n. Not even in a place like this; no son-of-a-bitch goddam f'n."

He means it, Pearce stood amazed, the guy really means it. "It's not a problem," he said.

"I hate that f'n."

"Well," Pearce said.

Robbie remained mute. Pearce was about to speak again when the boy said, "Hi, Shine."

"Them urinals I sent over get here okay?" the man asked Pearce.

"They're still downstairs," Pearce said. "They're pretty heavy and —"

"Were they a damaged shipment, hon?" Lucy interrupted.

"Nothin' wrong with them. I'll go get them."

"No it's —" Again Lucy cut in on Pearce, but she didn't seem to be speaking to Shiner so much as making an announcement when she said, "I thought you'd hurt yourself carrying that fridge up my stairs."

Shiner grunted.

"We can get some guys to help," Pearce said, resisting a compulsion, one he felt was expected, and which he resented, to thank Shiner again for helping the club out.

"Two other men couldn't get that fridge up those stairs." Lucy stood up, the rustling of her dress now the focus of the room. She moved behind the chairs to stand beside Shiner, who did not touch her. Pearce had never seen him touch her.

A machine-gun rattle filled the room. Robbie had gone over to the speed bag. With so few people in the room, and with the silence that had preceded it, the noise detonated off the hardwood floors.

Leaning down — she came up to his shoulder — Shine mouthed something to Lucy. Pearce thought it was little bitch or little girl. The two of them turned to leave the gym.

The noise continued, Robbie working the bag with the force and timing of a man, while Pearce stood there.

CHAPTER 2

THE OTHER BOXER WAS TAPPING his gloves together quickly.

"You're eager to get going, eh?" Pearce said, reluctant to handle his mouthpiece. He slipped it in.

The boy made a noise of assent, between a grunt and an exhalation.

"Now look," Pearce explained, "you're older and bigger than Rob. I want a sparring session, not a war. You pull your punches." He spoke reasonably and respectfully, but wondered if that was the right thing to do; he felt he was more willing the kid to understand than being listened to.

The boy nodded.

Applying Vaseline, Pearce kept doubting his judgement. This kid was close to full-grown now, and he found himself reluctant to smear his unshaven cheeks, concentrating on the brow ridge and forehead. "You're *sparring*," he emphasized.

"Uh-huh," like a cough.

Fastidiously, Pearce widened his fingers across the

rough face; he smiled flatteringly. "You're a lot bigger and older. This is a test for Rob."

There's something wrong with me, he thought, I should feel sorry for this kid. Was it the red-rimmed eyes, the way he talked: Mongoloid, just a touch? No one came to the gym more often, no one was more dedicated. Worrying about Rob winding up like this was nonsense; the boy was born the way he was. But the eyes, always pink around the edges, bloodshot — at this moment Pearce was not being heard.

"And a test for you too, Tommy," he emphasized. "You have a lot of skill." Pearce made himself slow down. "I don't want anyone to get hurt. You know what to do."

There was no response.

Pearce looked right at him, brought his face right up to his as if they were between rounds. "It's a test for both of you."

There was a perfunctory jerk of Tommy's head. His gloves kept slapping together.

"Take it easy, okay?" Pearce said. "You don't want to leave everything in the gym."

With a pat to the boy's headgear, Pearce got down. He looked over at Jimmy McSween, friend, "assistant," Robbie's co-trainer and cornerman. Shaking his head to show reluctance at this sparring, Pearce got back a big smile and the thumbs-up. So Pearce spread his arms wide, indicating both helplessness and too big. With a wave Jimmy dismissed all concerns, pushed the buzzer and yelled, "Time!"

Robbie wanted to touch gloves, but Tommy went right to the centre of the ring, planted as if he was going to hit a heavy bag, lifted his lead leg to his toes, and whistled a left hook. A mere motion with his right and he fired again.

"Hey!" Pearce yelled. Robbie didn't get caught, but the punches crossed his forearms.

Robbie leaned into him. Tommy kept throwing: hooks, but not looping hooks; he threw curving power punches that gave the impression no one could withstand them. Except they weren't quite getting through. Red blotches appeared just below Robbie's ribs, and a long streak across his upper back.

"I'm getting up there," Jimmy said.

When he reached them the boys were headgear to headgear, Robbie covering up completely, nearly ducking when he wasn't holding, his body being shaken as Tommy tried to pull his arm free — then did and socked.

"Hold on." Jimmy tried to separate them, but now Tommy, eyes blank, held on. "What's wrong with you guys?" Jimmy said. "You trying to kill each other? Box."

As soon as they were apart Tommy threw furiously again: Rob caught them on his shoulders and gloves and the top of his head; he staggered a little from the shock.

"What ya doing, throwing shots like that?" Jimmy said to Tommy. "Come on. Learn something. Box."

Going to a neutral corner, Jimmy leaned back, indicating he wasn't going to referee.

Pearce waved at Jimmy. "Get in there."

"No." Jimmy frowned, watching, motionless.

The boys stood apart from each other, Robbie with his hands up now like an open, classic boxer, Tommy peering over his gloves peek-a-boo style, bobbing and rolling even though he was the taller fighter.

They exchanged hard jabs, and closed again.

"Hey!" Pearce yelled.

Tommy got his left loose again and hooked three times fast to Robbie's headgear, high up.

Robbie came back with an uppercut, and an arc of saliva, clinging to Tommy's mouthpiece, flew out.

"Jesus!" Jimmy picked the mouthpiece off the canvas. Tommy seemed ready to go on without it; Robbie stepped back. "Hold on," Jimmy yelled. He rinsed the mouthpiece off. When he put it back in Tommy's mouth the boy immediately started to punch again, hitting Robbie with a right after Robbie had jabbed; the counterpunch hit Rob full in the face and his nose immediately started to bleed from both nostrils.

Afterward both Pearce and Jimmy wondered why they hadn't stopped it there, at least to clean Rob up. And maybe that was when they both forgot about the time.

Once again, in close, Tommy gathered himself and hooked; he seemed so much the stronger of the two. Robbie tried to spin him, to make him follow through in the direction of his punch and go off balance, and got clubbed twice on the ear.

No headgear and the ear would have been ruined, Pearce thought, a bunch of grapes. He watched, not liking the hard punches; later he realized he had stopped thinking.

Leaving his corner, dancing around, Jimmy jerked both hands at the fighters as if he was throwing little electric currents their way, hesitant, excited. Rob grabbed at Tom, trying to get the thumbs of his gloves where he could rub them back and forth over the tendons between Tommy's biceps and forearm. Where had he learned that?

It was no good; Tommy came up with an uppercut and the punch got turned so that the heel of his glove got Rob on the nose. More blood, and as Robbie leaned on Tommy's shoulder to give him some of it, Tom lifted his shoulder sharp and caught Rob on the nose again. The blood didn't smear much on Tommy's oily sweat.

He's never been in like this, Pearce thought, and didn't move. "No, no," he said quietly, as if correcting children, but didn't interfere, feeling his heart race but also feeling that he was in a trance. He pulled at the belt of his trousers, aware that he could hardly curl his hands. Where had Tommy gotten such force?

Then Robbie began to put his punches together, and instead of single, hard efforts, or throwing a left, then a right, he threw one, two, hook, coming back to his balance, tentatively finding a rhythm.

"Get back," Pearce said softly.

Still magically darting his hands, Jimmy circled on his toes.

Tommy jammed Robbie in the mouth, and the younger boy's lip started to come up. Doubling on his hook, Tommy hit Robbie in the right eye, twice. Unbelievably, Robbie started to bounce and sway and throw from all directions, coordinating punches: left, right, left hook, right, uppercut. And Robbie pulled the punches slightly, getting off on Tommy but not following through hard, working on a series: one two three four five, snap, gather and then again one two three . . . Later, wondering why he had not stepped in at the start, Pearce did not lie to himself and say he expected Robbie to come back the way he had. He had just stood there amazed.

"Oh, look at him sing, look at him wail," Jimmy said.

Then, as in those battles where an audience will roar at what fighters are capable of, but in which there is some confusion in the noise, a thread of dismay in the approval — the courage had gone too far, a limit passed — Tommy came back again. He snapped short rights to Robbie's ribs; the impact was transferred to Robbie's feet. Getting space, Tommy tried for Robbie's liver, but hit his abdomen. Again a tremor went down Rob's legs. No more could be done — Tommy put a glove on Robbie's neck and pulled him forward so their heads clashed.

"Shit," said Pearce.

Slipping forward, Rob leaned on Tom's shoulder again. It seemed he would slip to his knees. Tom rabbit-punched him.

"Goddam brain stem!" Jimmy removed the paw of Tom's glove from Rob's neck.

On the break Tom hit Rob in the face.

"Break clean!" Jimmy said.

Tom spit at Robbie.

"Christ." Spinning on Tommy in outrage, Jimmy drove at him with his face, as if challenging the boy to hit him.

Rob's arms fell, he backed off, but Tommy stepped around Jimmy, and Rob put his hands right back up and punched.

Looking all around the edge of the ring, as if confusedly searching for the buzzer, Jimmy stopped himself and barked, "Knock him out. Ah, knock him out!"

Pearce yelled.

The boys punched. Tommy hooked again, stumbled.

After he completed each punch, Tommy did not have any head movement; he'd lacked it all through the round. Now, taking a half step in, Rob raised his left shoulder and dropped his right fist down and swung it up so it smashed into the side of Tommy's static head, on the jaw.

"He ain't fancy now," Jimmy shouted.

Rob gathered to do it again, got the punch away, but because Tommy was falling he missed and hit him on the temple, protected by the headgear. Jimmy caught Tommy, put his arms around him. "That's enough."

"I'm not going down," a sob like a moan, stubbled chin covered with wet and mucus, mouth full of black from the mouthpiece, and blood.

"That's enough." Jimmy hugged him.

Robbie dropped back again, but not far. He put his hand out and touched Tommy's glove.

The older boy was breathing like he had asthma.

"Suck it up, son, suck it up," Jimmy said. He looked down at Pearce. "Let him finish the round?" It was advice more than a question.

"What about the time, it's time," Pearce said.

"Oh." Jimmy again searched around for the buzzer.

"Never mind," Pearce said.

"Okay." Jimmy looked intently at Tommy. "Suck it up," he said, "and finish it off."

Robbie waited, Tommy put his hands up, they boxed formally, technically, for a minute or so more.

Neither threw hard. Jimmy spoke a little, giving instruction, then, letting the noise run on too long, he sounded the end.

◪

In his pyjamas, the house feeling as polished as the moonlight that reflected in the glass of water by his bedside, Pearce thought of the feelings he experienced at fights.

There was the time a boy from the club had gone to the university for an exhibition and was put in with a — *goof* was the rounder's word, it got the fixed smile, but not the denial, with no room for conscience — a goof who came out windmilling with viscous intensity: absolutely inappropriate anywhere, and especially when they'd gone out of their way to provide him an opponent. When asked about it later the student gave his sharp grin and said, "I wanted to knock him out. That's what boxing's about, isn't it?" No, it wasn't, not in that situation, against a boy so much smaller; and the spoiled jerk didn't get his knockout. He was made to look bad, if not bad enough.

Some justice there.

And Jimmy at his Canadian lightweight championship, with the cut in his scalp, thank God he had a brushcut, having been low blowed and fouled but ready to tear in and finish, that one moment with him so eager to go with his left so far back it looked like the arm was being held on to, restrained: Jimmy's hook was followed through by his forearm and Pearce had yelled, "Crush his skull!"

Morality plays, the fighters our surrogates; the deepest emotions, but simple.

It hadn't been like that today.

Getting out of bed, Pearce paused and nudged around for his slippers; the thought of going into the corridor kept him where he was. Maybe he had simplified too much, stripped the house down too much. But it wasn't just neat and not clean, like some old bachelor's, with the scum underneath the shaving implements lined up like soldiers.

A foot touched his flattened moccasins. What was he going to do?

Was it a mistake to be this alone? But it had been the same when his mother was alive, at least at the end; for a long time really. The same place, yet great, great change. When had he discovered the secret pleasure of getting into clean sheets? As a teenager? Having never really lived with his "lady friend," Katy, was this his true sensuality? And that is what Katy had become in the end, just a friend. Pearce smiled with a little sadness and patted the cold crisp sheet at the other side of the bed. But then he realized he was happy enough, and that he always liked the sheets tucked in tight. The other side of the bed was nicely firm.

So disturbing what had gone on today, the adults' . . . not neutrality, nor paralysis, but watching. Aspects of the morality play were there, even if Tommy hadn't meant to do what he had done, but they were not a real factor. What they had done was leave the kid on his own, and Pearce had not even considered it. They'd just left him.

His nose was broken now.

Was Jimmy not checking the buzzer deliberate? No. Yet there are no accidents — at least like that.

Pearce imagined the house creaking, but there was only silence. He imagined the waxed hardwood of the second floor hallway, nightlit. He pictured what the kitchen would be like if he went there. Well, he had to get up.

Rob's nose had been broken.

CHAPTER 3

"GO FIRST CLASS, or don't go at all," Jimmy said loudly. The good humour he put in his voice made his vowels sound large, unexpectedly resonant in the quiet interior of the car. Behind him sat Robbie, his right hand resting lightly on the tackle box in which Jimmy carried his compressors, bandages, Q-Tips, swabs, sponge, Vaseline, and coagulants.

"Got your game face on." Pearce, who was driving, glanced around. He noticed Robbie using the red cut box as an arm rest and said, "That your department back there?"

Lucy stirred between the two men. "Could you open the window a crack?" Since they'd left Toronto she'd been wetting her lips and shifting, nearly imperceptibly, but so frequently that Robbie pushed his knee into the upholstery directly behind her.

"Stop it," she said, without turning around.

"What?" Robbie said.

"Hold on." Pearce felt around for an automatic button on the control panel by the door.

"I'll get it," Jimmy said, and the car became much noisier, wind whistling by the edge of the glass.

"I wonder why they put the highway through all this fruit land," Pearce said. "There's not that much of it in Canada. Fruit land, I mean."

Robbie still noticed his mother's dress rustling. Leaning forward, he pressed more forcefully with his knee into the yielding material.

"Oh stop it!" Lucy turned to confront him.

"How far we got to go?" the boy asked.

"Not too far now." Pearce spoke to Lucy, although she had not mentioned distance the whole trip. The lake was off to the left on this stretch, as pale as he imagined the Caribbean; there was a beach, a shelf of shale, black willow by a creek. And over the water towards the Unite States that Southern Ontario haze. "Hard to get a breath," he said and frowned. The air flew by and buffeted the car; it wasn't humid inside at all.

"Shiner was born in Niagara Falls." Running her tongue over her lips again, which gave her lipstick a bright sheen, Lucy rolled her head in a distracted way.

"That right." Now Pearce found himself glancing at her feet, and wondered, since she always seemed so dressed, why she didn't wear higher heels. Now why are we talking about Shiner? he thought. Let's talk about her. "You from Toronto?"

"I was born in Port Dalhousie."

"No!" Pearce said, and instantly recognized how patronizing he sounded. "Close to here," he added, but that didn't work either.

Lucy didn't seem to notice.

"You go over the river much?" Jimmy jumped in.

"How do you know that expression?" Lucy asked with animation. Her curiosity appeared to refresh her, and she was paying attention to Jimmy.

"Well, I knew that," Jimmy said. "I'd heard that. I think an aunt of mine used it."

"What, over the river, to the States?" Pearce said, but he was ignored even further. He wondered if it was such a good idea having her along. But what choice did they have? When she'd said, "Take Shiner's car," her hand rested briefly on his forearm. "He wants you to take the big Mercury. Better on the highway and it will make things easier for Robbie." Pearce, reasonably, believed what she said had merit. Of course he'd agreed! Now he regretted the enthusiasm he'd shown.

When they went to pick up the car, and the young lad, there she was — "Shiner said you can't take the car unless I go with you."

"That's fine. I see." He had not objected, even though he hadn't expected her to accompany them; it was never discussed. Always it had been assumed that this would be Robbie's first trip away from home. A kid like him had never been to camp or anything like that.

Now Pearce recalled how Lucy had looked as if she'd expected opposition, there'd been a strange defiant look on her face, because it was touched with a kind of self-pitying panic. Her wide, startled eyes had looked past him.

"That's fine," Pearce had said. Was she going to cry? No, she would never cry. The emotion was stronger, more desperate, than that.

Hair lighter than ever, a red vinyl belt around the

waist of her yellow sun dress, Lucy quickly slid into the front seat.

When he was behind the wheel Pearce asked, "Shiner isn't worried about insurance or anything, is all that okay?"

"Robbie can sit in the back" was how she'd answered.

And now they were almost there, to Robbie's first real test. The Niagara Falls Boxing Club was a good venue, and they could take their time getting back after the fight, if it went well. Or they could bang back full speed if he lost; but that would not happen, Pearce felt. It couldn't.

With his confidence up from knowing about "over the river," Jimmy started to tell a story. "Did you know that when Vinnie Canzerotti went on his honeymoon his mother-in-law went with them?"

"The guy's not even married." Pearce gripped the wheel. They'd be there soon.

"He was. And they went to Niagara Falls for the honeymoon. That's what made me think of it."

"Who's Vinnie Canzerotti?" Robbie asked.

"It doesn't matter," Lucy said, touching her hair.

"The old lady said she'd never seen the Falls, hadn't been anywhere since getting off the boat, and it was a chance for her to go."

"So who was more disappointed after that trip," Pearce asked, "the bride or the mother-in-law?"

Lucy continued to push at her hair with an open hand.

"Did they all stay in the same room?" Robbie asked.

Pearce smiled.

"Never mind," Lucy said.

Jimmy grinned. "Yeh, you got it."

"We've all got our own rooms," Pearce said.

"That's not what I'm saying," Jimmy said. "Don't get fussy."

"Who'd ever marry Vinnie?" Pearce asked, and steered them off the highway.

Rotating almost completely around, Lucy examined her son. "You okay, honey?"

"Yeah." Robbie sat back. "Turn around."

She hesitated, then did as he asked. "His father used to call the back seat Robbie's department," she said to Pearce. "'That's your department,' Will would say."

"Is that right," Pearce said. "How old was Will when he died?"

"Fifty-two."

"That's young," Pearce said. "And it's too soon for a young lad to lose his father."

"Will was an older father," Lucy said.

"But still," Pearce said. "Fifty-two isn't old."

"It's been many a moon since you seen fifty-two," Jimmy said.

"We'll each have our own rooms at the George," Pearce said.

◢

"This is not the kind of hotel you're used to." Pearce looked around as they stood in the lobby of an old building; doors to a bar, a draft room, and a dining room led off it. They were all closed. "But I —"

"My father used to travel a lot," Lucy said. "I'd go with him."

"Around Southern Ontario? The Niagara Peninsula?"

"He always said hotels were the best places to eat."

"A hot roast beef sandwich and a cup of coffee," Pearce said. "We aren't talking the Royal York here."

"He didn't drink coffee. He was English."

"From England?"

"'Now, Lucy,' Dad'd say in that way of his, 'Now, Lucy, do you understand? Do you understand, now?'" She walked away from Pearce, heels clicking on the polished floor of the lobby. "A hot roast beef sandwich is always a good choice," she spoke over her shoulder, quoting her father, then asking for her key.

"I'll bunk in with Jimmy," Pearce called after her, not moving.

After they had all checked in — Robbie would have a cot in the room with his mother — Pearce went to the gym to check things out. He'd told Robbie to nap, and wondered whether he'd be able to, imagining Lucy fixing her face in front of a mirror while the kid curled away from her, on the bed. Too bright in the afternoon. If she put on perfume in a small space like that it could make him sick. But how did he know what she'd do? He'd like to see himself. And who even knew if Robbie was one of those fighters who could nap?

What a day it turned out to be. The sky had lifted, and though he could see a mist from the river, which he did not bother going out of his way to look at, it was the kind of crystal weather that took away his headaches. He could hear the Falls, and thought he sensed water in the air from the spray. An optimism he told himself he shouldn't trust overcame him, one that had nothing to do with going to the gym, checking the canvas and turnbuckles, even making sure Robbie had a reasonable opponent.

He went along, an older man in a hat. River light sloped up a narrow street to his right; above him was a blue immensity to which he did not lift his face but which seemed to fill his life.

CHAPTER 4

THEY WAITED IN THE CORNER, Pearce and Jimmy leaning forward, looking up as if anticipating the pop of a starting gun. In the light from the ring their faces were yellow and waxen.

Above them, foreshortened, shaking his arms downward, Robbie scuffed his shoes. His shining Vaselined face, the simian protuberant lips from the mouthguard, made his equipment, the headgear and gloves, seem very big.

Across the ring Robbie's opposition was eager to come out.

"That's the widest shoulders and back I ever saw on a teenager," Jimmy said to Pearce.

"That's all right," Pearce said, with a confidence that was just slightly different from anything he had felt in boxing. He'd been uncannily confident before, but there was a unique little shiver of joy in this; even if he was to be unpleasantly surprised he would remain serene. And he would not be surprised.

"If that boy's a novice then so am I," Jimmy said.

"He's got shoulders and arms like a heavyweight."

"At a hundred and twelve pounds?"

"He don't have much legs."

It was exactly what he'd worried about, Pearce thought, staring at the rash of acne across the opponent's back and down his shoulders: they had picked someone for Robbie who was technically a novice, just short of the required number of fights to move up, but whose whole purpose was to administer a beating. And the beating was directed at Jimmy and Pearce, for all the victories their club had had here. It was a hell of a way to go, Pearce thought, overmatching a kid like Rob. But they'd heard about him. I foresaw this, he told himself. I'm startled as I always am and I shouldn't be, but it won't make a difference. If I have to I'll jump in there myself, without indignation.

"It won't be necessary," Pearce said to Jimmy.

"What?"

"It's okay," Pearce said.

"What's okay?"

The bell went.

"I think I've seen this kid before," Jimmy said.

"That's all right."

"He poses, Robbie," Jimmy called up. "You can lead."

"Leave it," Pearce said, and that's when he thought he noticed a familiar camelhair coat behind the seats at the back of the club. And a shorter man that he knew as well, standing back there, a squat man with a dark, swollen face.

"I hope the boy doesn't see him," Pearce said to Jimmy.

"Who?"

"Forget it." With a nod of his head Pearce directed their attention to the ring.

A punch had not been thrown. A half circle, Robbie jabbing into the air for form's sake, then, right away — Pearce and Jimmy couldn't tell if it was intentional — the other boy was leaning back on the ropes, hands by his face and elbows against his sides.

"There's nothing for him to cover up against," Pearce said.

"Don't go in there," Jimmy shouted.

But it's the other kid in the danger zone, Pearce thought. "Rob has the range," he told Jimmy.

Bent at the waist, bobbing like he had been taught, Robbie moved laterally, sideways and back, sideways and back, cutting off escape, but again the moves were formal, his opponent wasn't trying to get away.

"Rob's slipping punches nobody's thrown," Jimmy said.

"Let's go," someone shouted, though the cry from the audience was half-hearted because there was, in the ring, in spite of the lack of action, a sense of the potential for furious, silent struggle.

Suddenly straightening up, seeing something no one else saw, Robbie punched. Again it was tentative; he hit hands.

"Why doesn't the other guy throw anything? What's he waiting for?" Jimmy threw out his hands; his voice pitched up.

"Take it easy," Pearce said, as positive as he had been before the bout, but beginning to wonder about the feeling. "Does either of them know what to do?" He smiled, trying to be detached, and decided to not let himself rule out being surprised.

"If you're built like that you know what to do," Jimmy said. But the other boy leaned back, almost as if he was waiting to be given an order.

"You know," Pearce said, "I'm starting not to like this either."

"That other kid's in there smiling like a goof," Jimmy said. "I think he's all screwed up."

Then, with an intensity that surprised everyone at the Niagara Falls Boxing Club, Robbie smacked him. Was it the sound or the intention that was so impressive? Pearce wondered, because a punch was no way to describe it. A belt was a little closer, there was something of that in the noise, but it didn't get the directed, ruthless force. For so many years he and Jimmy had casually talked about, and heard talk about, knockout punches. The language was designed, intentionally, everybody accepted it, to hide the violence that could be in a blow. And the description worked: most blows really were just that, technical shots, punches. But what happened here could only be described as some kind of strange slap, maybe the way you'd think of one kid hitting another, but with an absolute finality in it that was designed to eliminate the other. Obliterate him. There was no bad intention here, Pearce felt, there was extreme, impersonal violence.

The other boy's face blurred. He was whacked again. There was no blood, though there seemed to be some kind of mist as his face distorted.

And there was that sound, or merely the impression of a sound — wet skull plates shifting, held together by the helmet? — the noise he'd heard as a boy when they put two mice in a cloth sack and swung them into a brick wall to kill them.

Had it been that bad?

The referee stepped in right away. No knockdown.

Jimmy shook his head. "I hadn't even noticed there was a ref in there."

"That's the fastest I've seen one interfere," Pearce said.

The fight was stopped.

"It's the right thing," Pearce said, nodding.

Protest at the stoppage came from the other corner, but it was pro forma. In spite of voices and some buzz the whole room was subdued.

The ring doctor climbed up to look in the eyes of the boy who had been hit. Short as the fighters, with black hair like a helmet and an Aztec face, he put his thumbs under the boxer's eyes, then slipped them sideways down his cheeks.

"Dr. Butterfingers," Jimmy said.

"Is that guy wearing a rug?" Pearce didn't ask anyone in particular.

The doctor turned away, agreeing with the decision to stop the fight. He went over to examine Robbie, again putting his thumbs on the face and again unable to pull the eyes any more open than they were. He stared, then nodded okay.

"I should hope so," Jimmy said. "He wasn't touched."

"He's hardly sweating," Pearce said.

Quickly, the noise in the room increased. Just another TKO. The shock, whatever the crowd had seen, or thought they had seen, was ignored, forgotten quickly. The referee raised Robbie's hand — he had stayed in a far part of the ring, not going over to Pearce and Jimmy.

"Good job," they both said when he did come back.

Robbie got down, Jimmy picked up the bucket and water bottle, and they moved aside to let the next group into the ring.

◤

It was Shiner whom Pearce had seen at the back of the gym, and now the big man came up with that tight, lopsided grin — Pearce thought of it as a tightening of his facial muscles — that showed yellow pearls of teeth in one corner of his mouth. They always look as false as the smile, by God, Pearce thought. But the boy beamed back.

"Maybe now you realize how well you did out there." Pearce stepped between Robbie and Shine, his back to Maclean, and tugged at Rob's gloves. "Let's cut these off right here."

As he ineffectively picked at the tape around Rob's wrists he waited to hear "Good fight" or "Congratulations" over his shoulder. Nothing happened.

The lad's been caught off guard, Pearce thought, getting a hint of Shiner's cologne. He's only just realized what he's done. I wonder if anyone else has. "We should get these off," he stressed.

"Uncle Shine." Robbie smiled, like he hadn't in the ring, like he hadn't days before the fight.

"This here's Rocco Canzanno," Shiner introduced his friend, the short man he had been standing with.

"How ya doin'?" Rocco said, his face too big for his body. His dark herringbone coat was too tight, but he wasn't fat. His face especially seemed too big because his nose had been spread, not broken or squashed, but pushed back while remaining bulbous, with wide nostrils. He wore a tweed cap and smiled, his teeth the colour of his coat.

"How do you guys know each other?" Pearce asked Shiner, then said, "Hello, Mr. Rocco."

"Hey," Rocco acknowledged with a self-congratulatory nod, which nevertheless included everyone else in it and made them all feel good. To create an even more sporty, instant familiarity, to show what a good guy he was and put everyone even more at ease, Rocco made a little self-deprecating reference to the respectful way Pearce had used his first name. "Mr. Rocco," he said, "the first shall be last."

"How's that?" Shiner said.

"That's how you go, right?" Pearce said.

"Yeah, yeah," Rocco said.

"Ex–flyweight champion of the world," Pearce explained to Robbie.

"Never champion," Shiner said.

"I fought for it," Rocco said with crinkly-eyed modesty.

"Do you still own the Rex Tavern?" Pearce showed his knowledge of Rocco Canzanno.

"I've done things that are a lot harder way of making money." Rocco kept smiling, still very friendly, but he wasn't showing his teeth any more.

Robbie nodded as if puzzled, which irritated Pearce, who felt he should have been more impressed with who Rocco was.

"Let's go." Pearce tried to stop himself being angry that Robbie had given Shiner a greeting that was not deserved.

Taking a step, his red hair and beige colours and

freshly shaven face giving an impression, if not an outright smell, of the outdoors, Shiner put his bulk between Pearce and Robbie, but he still didn't say anything.

Pearce felt Shiner and Rocco, standing there tugging at their overcoats, were a little too pleased, were taking too much credit themselves for Robbie's victory. But that was always the way.

Finally, with just a hint of shyness, just a slight turning away as if even he must hesitate and share the humour with himself before mentioning it, Shiner said directly into Robbie's face, "That guy won't need an enema after a beating like that."

"Wait a minute." Crinkling his face in disbelief, but careful enough to show he was contending a point, Pearce said, "There weren't any body shots thrown."

He was ignored.

If he was taken aback Rocco didn't show it, but he did say, "I never heard of anyone needing no enema after a fight."

"You never heard of taking an enema to feel good?" Shiner stared right at Robbie. "A good enema."

"Well, I've heard of that," Rocco said. "But not around boxing. You're talking about health!"

"Fighters are in good shape," Pearce said.

Shiner turned to Rocco. "It's an old remedy."

"Well, I don't need it," Robbie said.

"You feel great, eh, kid?" Rocco didn't give Robbie a chance to answer. "You know the doctors couldn't believe me, they couldn't understand. Before the world championship the doctor in my corner said, 'Roc, your heart's hardly pumpin'. What's the matter with you?'"

"That's unusual," Pearce said.

"I was just ready, it didn't bother me. They couldn't believe it."

There was a pause, and before any of the others could respond Rocco said, "I loved it, eh."

"Was Savat's heart going?" Pearce asked. Rocco had fought Savat Bissonnette three times, and won once, but in a non-title bout.

"Certainly," Rocco said, showing he took no offence if this was a reference to his defeats.

"You got to know that Frenchman very well," Pearce said.

"Frenchman," said Rocco. "He was from the East End. He was a waiter at the Gerrard House."

"Well, you certainly made him dislike boxing," Pearce said.

"You see those fights?" Rocco asked.

"No."

Rocco turned to Robbie. "You're like me, eh, kid?"

"How's that, sir?" Robbie cocked his head.

"Heh. Sir," Shiner said. "Your mother taught you good."

With real warmth Rocco interrupted Rob's puzzlement. "You looked pretty cool and collected up there, son."

"Really?" Rob said. "Sometimes it feels like I'm not thinking."

"Hey, that's the way, stay within yourself. Then you really can know what you're doing."

"You can really follow instructions then," Pearce said, and laughed.

"That's right," Rocco said, seriously. "You know you're okay, then your corner can help you."

"Here's his mother," Shiner said.

CHAPTER 5

WHEN ROCCO ARRIVED at his cottage he took his fishing rod off the screened veranda and immediately went down to the dock, not bothering to change his clothes or unlock the place. He'd stopped for some leeches on the way, and saw that the boy was already there, by himself, waiting.

It couldn't have just been the kid's potential that made him invite the bunch of them up here, to this country place — well, it wasn't really the country, just a summer house on Lake Simcoe, about an hour's drive north of Toronto. Jackson's Point, Keswick, it felt like the little places nearby would never be overrun, no matter how far the suburbs expanded. The landscape around here was different, it seemed to breathe differently — that's it, the landscape, especially at night, breathed. Huge, quiet, it exhaled. Boy, am I a city boy, Rocco stopped and smiled at himself, wondering about slipping on the lawn in his smooth-soled shoes. He tried to think about what he was doing. Instead he thought about where he was.

His dock was painted black, and the boards covering the rocks and pilings sloped like a skirt so he could sit with his feet pushed comfortably out in front of him. Lake Simcoe was hazy, the landless horizon and all the water in between holding not a glare but a diffusion of light, concentrations of it in a haze near the surface. Even in winter the lake had a different feel than what Rocco thought of as the North: Muskoka, Haliburton where he hunted deer, especially those camps where he'd gone with the Vetere brothers — sitting on the goddam logging road north of Sault Ste. Marie for two days waiting for help, drinking from a puddle. It's where he'd had his first heart attack. He couldn't be sure about that, but it was where the heart thing started.

His wife didn't want him to go hunting any more — just the way she'd glanced over at him from the side of her eye when he'd mentioned it this summer. She was fluffing cushions on the cottage porch.

"All right." He had drawn the word out. "Let me think about it."

Around here was different. There were farms and even driving down the sanded road to his place in January with the cedars in the field corners, nearly black against the snow, and nobody around for miles, it was not what he thought of as empty. Not like farther north.

With a sentimental finality that scared and thrilled him at the same time, because he didn't quite believe in it, like his own death, Rocco said to himself: Buying this place was one of the best things I ever did.

Still reluctant to move, he took the cover off the bait container and watched the leeches fluttering in the clear water of the white cup.

Then he looked up again. Robbie was walking up and down, in a long-sleeved plaid shirt buttoned right up to the neck, a fall shirt on a summer day, pathetic really, but the kid had probably never been out of the city in his life, just like it had been for him at that age. Nobody better tell a tough kid like that he didn't look right, because he could really punch. Boy, he could punch.

Still, had he really needed to ask the whole crazy clan up here — Pearce and that trainer who was either cross-eyed or punchy and Shiner and the mother? It was only for the day, that was what the good thing, as he'd repeated all too often, you could come up for just the day. Rocco wondered if he hadn't bothered to change clothes because he didn't want Rob to feel uncomfortable, so he'd fish beside him in a business suit. Or was it to let them all know they were close to home and had to get back? Neither one — he'd been in a real hurry to reach the boy, and yet now he stood still.

Why didn't he move? Was it thinking about the way Robbie had looked at him after the fight, just for a minute, so goddam appreciative or something, clear? He'd had one good word for him and the kid kept saying, "Thanks, Mr. Rocco. Thank you."

For what?

While the boy had been busy thanking him the mother had come over and piped in, "Call him Mister."

"That's what he's been doing," Rocco said and looked her over: dressed for the evening, in black, at an afternoon fight, with a hat and a veil. The same height as Rocco and her son, but she seemed smaller than both of them. There was the strain on her face of public performance that she didn't seem aware of, but for which the others had to account. Not dazed so much as a little distracted, slow on the uptake because she was involved with something else. Herself?

"Mum," Rob had said.

Shine had laughed and tried to take over. "You going to a funeral, little girl?"

"She's already been to an execution," Jimmy said to the big man. "We'll forget the funeral."

Nervously, he wasn't sure why, Rocco started to brush off the breast of his coat, as if he had crumbs on it. "That's right." He stopped and faced them all. "Impressive."

"By God, yes," Pearce said.

"Thanks again," Robbie said.

"This is *Mr.* Rocco." Shiner took Lucy by the elbow and steered her so she faced the ex-fighter close up.

Was that where the fishing invitation came in? Roc couldn't remember, and in the heavy, tiring outdoor air closed his eyes, trying to recall everything. When had the boy talked about about seeing a picture of Shiner in a buckskin with a — it must have been a trout? Shiner hadn't even known Robbie had seen the photo, it had been at some rich bastard's preserve, something like that. The invitation must have come close to then, for sure, the kid standing there in his headgear and his entourage around him like a horse-shoe, that was when Rocco had asked the whole kit and caboodle of them to come up fishing. No, only the boy for fishing, the rest could come on up to the lake. What the hell.

They'd all show up, he was sure of that, but now

he could see only the young guy. And that's who he really felt like talking to. So why the hesitation? Down Rocco went, pushing himself to slide a little on the grass.

◥

"You're here," Rocco said to the boy. "Would you like to train at a health farm some place like this? Up in the Catskills? Rocky Marciano's farm?"

"Is that what you did?"

"No." Rocco smiled.

"Say, Mr. Rocco," Robbie said. "Thanks for having me."

"Naw." There it was, that gratitude again — whatever he was thanking Rocco for it had been given freely enough. And it was not just that the kid could get a following, like Rocco had told Shiner; Robbie wasn't no Mexican or something like that and he could get community interest in Toronto which you had to have. And it wasn't that he was a special kind of boy, the kind who would really work for it. He was. Maybe it was that he was just a kid, just a simple enough kid. Appreciative. "Where's your folks?"

"Shiner isn't my dad."

"I know that. But you didn't get up here by yourself."

"They went shopping."

"Shopping. At the crossroads?"

Robbie shrugged.

"Where's Pearce and what's-his-name?"

"Jimmy and Stu are coming up later."

"Later. They missed half the day as it is. Sit down, sit down."

The boy was good company. He took delight in

watching the tiny fish under the pilings, in waiting for the bass, and he seemed to want Rocco to catch all the fish. They didn't talk much boxing, but when they did Rocco, strangely, with small oppressive distaste, remembered the light in those days, and sweat dark on hardwood floors. "I don't care if the sun comes out," he said to Rob. "It's nice anyway."

There were a few sincerely interested questions from Robbie about Savat, and about Rocco's heartbeat again. The lad's amazement couldn't help but make Rocco say in an evasive, but honestly pleased-with-himself, way, "You remember that, huh?"

Then they saw Lucy, standing above them on the road. She was wearing yellow shorts and a blouse with epaulettes that was tied in the front so that her midriff was bare.

Rocco waved her down. She joined them and walked tentatively out onto the dock, feeling her way slightly. The boards are close together, Rocco thought, what's the problem?

"Mum," Robbie said.

"Sit down, sit down," Rocco said. "Where's Shine?"

"How come you're here?" Robbie asked. "How come you're back?"

"Shine dropped me off," she said, then explained for Rocco. "The three of us came up this morning together. Jimmy and Pearce will come in a separate car."

"So I been told," Rocco said.

"Well, when we arrived and you weren't here" — with her head tilted down she peered at Rocco — "we left Robbie to wait and Shine I drove over to the crossroads to get a few things. Then we cruised by again and saw your car in the driveway and Shine let me out. He went on by himself to see if he couldn't find a liquor store."

"I got plenty at the house," Rocco said.

"It wouldn't be just for today." She knelt beside them.

"Sit down, right down," Rocco said. "That's okay."

Lucy, a little awkwardly, let her rear bump as she sat and gave a yelp of surprise, or relief.

Robbie looked away.

With her legs resting, angled out on the flared pilings beside theirs, Lucy reached and took her shoes off. "Feels nice," she said.

"You could go for a swim," Rocco said.

"My bathing suit is still in the car, when you weren't here at —"

"Did you see Stu and Jimmy anywhere?" Robbie cut in.

"Not yet." Lucy's voice was singsong, and she extended her feet, pointing her toes. "Did you thank Mr. Rocco?" she said to Robbie.

"That's all he does," Rocco said. "We're fine. We've had a good time."

"Swimming's great," Lucy said. "But a lot of the time when you go swimming you don't swim, if you know what I mean."

"You can swim here," Rocco said. "It slopes out gradual."

"When he was little my girlfriend and I used to take Robbie with us when we went to the tank in Toronto. We hardly went in the water."

"What, the municipal pool?" Rocco asked.

Lucy nodded. "The tank. He was a joy."

"Mum," Robbie said.

"He was funny," she insisted. "With all those different figures around —" Lucy shuddered — "we'd ask the kind *he* liked. He had no ideas about stretch marks or what having a baby will do! It was fun. That was before the bikini."

"Is that right," Rocco said.

"I wonder if I should go look for Shiner's car," she said.

"We'll be fine," Rocco said. "Go ahead."

Using Rocco's shoulder, Lucy pushed herself up, letting out a little self-conscious groan of exertion, but as soon as she was up she said, "He knows where we are," and sat back down again.

"It's all right, Mum," Rob said.

Flexing her thighs and doing a little flutter kick, Lucy said, "I'm embarrassed, the nail polish on my toenails is beginning to peel off."

"That's okay," Rocco said.

"I didn't think about it when I was coming. Doing them's a pain anyway." As she relaxed again, Lucy's bare heel knocked against Rocco's polished loafer.

"Them feets okay," Rocco said.

◪

By dusk two bass lay plump and stiff between Rocco and Robbie. They'd kept them because Rocco said the kid had to have a taste, though Lucy had insisted she wasn't going to clean them. Nobody'd asked her to.

There was a smear on the legs of the older man's business suit, and a stain on the dock. Rocco smiled to himself because he felt the dead fish were part of a little group that sat and waited for the sun to go down.

Rain would wash that mucus off the wood. Now, as

dusk began, the haze of daylight thickened and it was getting hard to see.

"We should go up to your mother and the others," Rocco said.

"You gave them the keys," Robbie said. "They're okay."

"That big one really fought," Rocco said.

"Both of them did. The pull from under the water is so strange, so deep. I never felt nothing like it."

Always it was a kind of shock when they hit, the smooth violence, and then what seemed the necessity to get them out of the water too fast. Better to be attached to that feel of muscle in a longer, slower way. They'd pulled these two out and laid them down and each one bounced — if they had flipped back in Rocco might not have stopped them. But they'd died quickly and joined them.

Bass like that were built like he was, Rocco thought, big shoulders even if they didn't have arms: sockers. Not like Savat had been built, and not like that boy Robbie. It wasn't the taller guys had reach, that wasn't so much it, but longer arms, if they could torque, get their body into it, meant they could punch too. It must have been a kind of leverage. He'd tried to explain it once by saying that getting hit by a guy with heavy hands was like being run into by a Mack truck at fifty miles an hour. But with another kind of puncher it was like getting whacked by a little Pontiac, but one that was going a hundred. Same result from guys who could hit. Maybe skinny Savat could only sting; Sugar Ray Robinson was built like Rob, though he was a little more slender, and he could punch. That's how the young boy's body was and only Christ knew what would happen if he put his punches together. He would be able to wail, not just stand there and bang.

I could hit, Rocco thought, but I had to do it a lot.

When Lucy had told them to take their shirts off Rocco had refused, saying "too old" and by God he was, and "I got a hairy back and a permanent tan. I'm yellow." But Rob had undone all his buttons and sat there for a while barechested under the heavy, sunless sky. Even so he looked as white as if he had never been outdoors, his skin the way it was when he'd stopped that guy with hardly breaking a sweat and was beginning to cool too fast — his torso suddenly blue in places, the waxen, shaped muscles touched with shadow.

He had so little fat on him he must have got cold easy. "You'll get chilled," Rocco had told him, with Lucy adding, "Put your shirt on."

Take it off, put it on, Rocco thought.

"Thanks, Mr. Rocco," the kid had said again.

But they hardly talked now, and sudden drops began to dimple the clear slate-blue surface of the lake. Down the shore it was impossible to see the boulders that jutted out, they were as grey as cloud, with a darkness at their centre.

"We better go up," Rocco said.

CHAPTER 6

A GOOD SOAK WAS WHAT SHE NEEDED. When Robbie was younger and she used to bring him into the bath with her she had never been able to take this kind of time. He was nearly a teenager now, of course, but she remembered him at that age — "just an eight-years-old boy" was how she put it. She couldn't really think of him as a teenager yet, and some things between them would never change.

Lucy closed her eyes. Then she wondered if she heard, or felt, the front door of the apartment bang. Shiner? She had an impulse to get up and lock the bathroom door, but she didn't move. The water was so hot and deep. They had never had this much hot water at the old apartment. She lay back and decided to wait a few more minutes before washing her hair. Maybe it was Robbie getting home early.

Even though he had been a little boy Robbie made such a fuss about taking baths with her, poking at the bumps on her spine and kicking her lower back. Grey water had sloshed past her hips.

So warm here. Even though it had been a sticky day they had not gone swimming at Rocco's cottage, somehow it would have been too cold. Brushing suds away from her breasts, Lucy looked at her freshly pedicured toenails protruding from the water. Candy-apple red, but it looked nice.

She thought of Rocco and Robbie on the dock; they were kind of cute, and he was a quiet man, somehow better looking once you got to know him. Rugged. Lucy thought of an English movie actor she liked, who was also short, and realized with quick irritation that Rocco didn't look like him at all. He looked like a pumpkin. No, he didn't. She closed her eyes, sank deeper, and relaxed.

Robbie was spending too much time at the gym, she decided. It was good for him to get away to a cottage, but not to go up there by himself, without her.

Not quite asleep, very conscious the water would grow tepid and she would have to get out, Lucy remembered the first time she had taken Robbie to a gym, not long after Will died.

He used to call their son a little truck, but she had been worried about his weight. Since then his body had changed so much.

Blond and chunky, and not much more than eight — his hair had darkened since — and the headgear Jimmy McSween strapped on him was too tight. They were not supposed to spar, but the helmet went on his sweet little face anyway and she looked at it and thought it seemed to push his face forward, to make it fatter and make it a target. That worried her. And he got into the ring and got knocked down right away, Pearce standing over him with the same pale chamois shirt he still wore tucked into pants that were riding too high — the way he still wore them. "Get up, Robbie," he'd said. "I'm not going to help you. You're not a punching bag." Then Pearce had looked over the ropes to where she was sitting and said, "They can't hurt each other with these sixteen-ounce gloves."

Robbie did get up and he put his hands by his face and charged at the other kid. He wound up in a corner and Pearce had said, "Punch out of there," and he had and Pearce said, "Stop."

Climbing down and coming right over to her, first thing, smiling, sweat beaded below his squinched-up eyes and also a little red mark below one eye. She said to him, "Are you okay, honey?"

"Yep, 'cept I got a headache, and I *used* to be the best reader in grade three."

How could a child think up a line like that? He was such an observant little boy, he must have noticed right away how Jimmy McSween slurred.

Pearce had followed behind Robbie, breaking one of his own rules and leaving the other boys alone in the ring for a moment.

"I like him," he said to her, and then added, holding up his hand, "I know, you're like all parents, but they really can't get hurt with those gloves."

"I wasn't that worried," she'd said. "I didn't say anything."

"He's got quite a chin," Pearce had said.

"Pardon?"

"He takes a good punch."

"I'm not sure that's the greatest virtue to have in the world," she'd said.

"I like him," Pearce had said again.

And he did like him. The time that man had spent with him. Of course he got something out of it too, becoming the trainer of Robbie Blackstone. And she was still worried about him getting hurt.

"Is that you?" Lucy hollered from the tub, knowing from the thumping and banging that it had to be Robbie — dropping his bag, never picking up.

"Yeah," she heard from the next room.

"I'm in the bath," she hollered.

No answer, which angered her, and made her determined to take her time and wash her hair properly and not rush. But she did wind up hurrying, and got out quickly, wrapping a towel around her head and another around her body. Holding the short towel in front of her with one hand, she rushed out of the bathroom to find Robbie in the kitchen, making himself something to eat. Lucy dripped on the floor. She almost slipped in her bare feet.

"Can't you answer?" she said.

"I did." He looked up from the bread he was spreading with peanut butter.

"You never answer."

Robbie went back to his snack. "I talked to Mr. Rocco," he said casually. "He came down to the gym and —"

"Rocco is his first name," she said irritably. "Why do you call him Mister?"

"You always say use Mister!"

That enraged her. "Why didn't you answer me!"

"I did. Anyway, he wants us to go fishing again. Me."

With his side turned towards her, wearing his singlet, and the muscles of his arms moving as he made his snack, Lucy was struck again by how much her little boy had changed. But the garment didn't flatter him, she thought, it really wasn't appropriate.

"Do you have to wear that Italian undershirt all the time?"

"It's warm out."

Changing her tone, Lucy said in a neutral voice, "You're still like me, you know, you've got those little fat pads at the front of your arms and they don't look good in a shirt like that." She stopped looking at him.

Robbie glanced down at the front of his shirt.

"No, no, by your armpits. I have to buy perspiration shields or else I'd ruin my blouses."

"Why are you saying that? Why are you comparing . . . ?"

Lucy moved to go away.

Robbie burst out, "What are you talkin'? What are ya talkin', fat sacs," as he pictured the grey, half-moon little pillows that he knew well.

"And you still go in there," she said stubbornly, looking at the seat of his sweat pants, "like I do." With her free hand she made a loose gesture by the side of her buttocks, indicating an indentation. Slightly unsure about what she was doing, she kept her arm away from her body.

Robbie went rigid. "This is bullshit," he said.

"Don't you talk to me like that."

"I didn't say nothin'!"

"What did you just say? You can't talk to me like that."

"Why not?"

"I'm your mother."

"Oh."

She sensed he was looking at her thighs, finding

something wrong with them, and Lucy was very conscious that all she had on was a towel. She took a step, and she thought Robbie was noticing that her flesh shook, which enraged her.

"Stop it," she spit.

"I'm not doin' nothin'!"

"Stop looking at me that way. You're looking at me funny."

"No I'm not." His forehead furrowed.

"You stop it!"

"I ain't doing nothin'!"

Now his face looked to her unnaturally white. It bothered her — it irritated and angered and repelled her. He *was* looking at her legs.

"Stop it," she said, then impulsively, "You can't go up to Rocco's any more."

"Why not?" Robbie's lip curled, he pulled his head backwards as if struck.

"He's a nice man but we're taking advantage of him," she said softly.

"How?" Rob asked. "I mean, he just said we could. He ain't getting nothing out of it."

"He's a nice man but —"

"He's not nice," Robbie said. "He's just . . ."

"He's an attractive man," Lucy said. "It's just . . ."

"He's not attractive." Robbie looked close to tears. "He's not attractive."

"You don't think he doesn't want to be part of your career?" she asked sharply.

"Career," Robbie said. "Fishing isn't my career."

"Don't you see," she said, and then: "I'll have to go with you."

"Why?"

"Stop looking at me like that!" She glanced down at her bare legs.

"I'm not looking at you!"

She stepped closer and slapped him. "Stop it!"

Bending his trunk as if slipping a punch, Robbie moved to the centre of the kitchen. His feet, spread in a boxing stance, never lost contact with the linoleum, and smeared the water Lucy had dripped.

"What you do that for?" he asked.

It seemed years since she had hit him. "I'm your mother," Lucy said emphatically.

"So what?"

Starting towards him, one arm raised, the other squeezing the towel at her chest into a knot, Lucy said, "Don't you —"

"Nay, hen, nay," Robbie whispered, and backed up. "Nay, hen, nay," he burst out.

She stopped.

"Nay, hen, nay." He half-heartedly put his left arm out in a jab to fend her off, his hand not quite in a fist. He was a distance away from her.

"What does that mean? Where'd you learn that?" Lucy was outraged.

"The Roc says to keep punchin'." He fluidly jabbed again.

Lucy clomped after him, but lowered her arm. "You can't talk to me like that. Who told you that, hen."

"Pearce," Robbie said, "but he don't say it about you." Laughing a bit, confused, backing up, he repeated, "Nay, hen, nay."

"Then Pearce —" She grabbed abruptly at her turban, which was slipping.

"Stick and move," Robbie said.

Then there was a bang at the front door of the apartment.

"Oh God," she said, "Shiner," and shouted, "Hel-lo."

Having backed away from her as far as he could, Robbie stopped and stared out the picture window. They were on the seventh storey, and he could see the roofs of houses below.

"Hello," Lucy yelled, tucking in a corner of the thick wet cloth on her head. "Don't you have your keys!" She started for their bedroom but then went to the door and looked through the peephole. There was another thump. "Just a minute." She twisted the lock and made her escape.

With a burlap sack in one hand and his other clenched at his side, Shiner strode in.

"Didn't you have your keys?" Robbie could hear his mother call.

"Uncle Shine." Rob turned to face him.

"Ore samples." Shiner hefted the bag to draw attention to it. Then he walked into the kitchen and, on his way to the bottle of rye Lucy always left standing beside the sink for him, dumped the contents. The rocks rolled and bumped; they were dusty and ochre-coloured and crumbly and stained the water on the floor.

"I wanted to ask you something," Robbie said, as if he had just thought of it.

"Yeah." If Shiner was surprised Robbie didn't leave as he usually did, he didn't show it.

"You know the trumpet."

"Yeah." He was filling nearly half a glass with rye, and turned on the tap.

"I play the trumpet, eh."

"Is that right." After he'd finished making his drink Shiner held it, untouched, at his waist.

"At school. Anyway, I was wondering if I should focus more on boxing or the trumpet."

His mother had encouraged him to ask Shiner things like this. Now he did want to know. And so he asked.

"Nobody ever knows who the guy is who plays the trumpet," Shiner said.

"That's what I thought," Robbie said. "What about if you solo?"

"Who knows who the guy is who plays the trumpet? But the guy who wins at track or . . . everybody knows." Shiner shrugged slightly as he said "everybody," both sharing something with Robbie, including him in the general knowledge of how it was, at the same time dismissing him and his naive concerns.

Lucy came out wearing slacks and a jersey, with a bandanna over her hair. Her lipstick was fresh and her makeup powdery on damp skin. Distracted, not quite tremulous over the fight with Robbie and the unexpected knock on the door, she said, "Look at the muck," and stared down at a muddy streak.

"Rio Algom," Shiner said. "It looks good. Real good."

She looked up suddenly. "Could you get Robbie a job up North for the summer?"

"What? Underground?" Shiner said.

"A job," she said.

"I don't know. I mean, he's what, how old? I don't know."

"He's too young to go away," she said decisively.

"You just wanted me to get him a job!" Shiner said.

"And now *Mr.* Rocco wants to take him fishing all the time," she said.

"I'll talk to the Roc," Shiner said. "He's good about the boxing."

"It's not about boxing," Robbie said.

"Who's going to clean up the muck?" Lucy asked.

"I don't give a shit," Shiner said.

"Look at the muck."

CHAPTER 7

PEARCE'S HOUSE HAD CHANGED so much since his mother died, yet what his friends, and others, commented on, over and over, was that he lived alone. Didn't they realize that the silence of his place was a consolation?

And he had never married. Priest or pervert, always with a dimension of pity: that was how he could feel treated. Katy and other lady friends, his happiness in what he had done to the place, to parts of his life, counted for next to nothing.

The family's old furniture was gone, all of it. Nearly empty rooms had been painted, and big new windows put in, some without drapes; rugs lifted and the floor polished. Nothing could brighten the hallway of a narrow, semi-detached place like this, but he'd tried. Well, it's their problem, Pearce thought, waiting in the kitchen for Robbie and Jimmy McSween, and I was no saint to come here and be with my mother in her last illness. But people did have a bit of a point: he might as well have lived in a bachelor pad for the number of rooms he really used.

Here was McSween, gazing around the dividing pillar on the front porch at his neighbour's veranda. What did he see there, why did he always do it? Pearce kept nothing outside, his porch was so open it felt like it had no roof; the neighbour's was dusty and cluttered, which interested McSween every time.

Pearce opened the door. "Jimmy, get in here."

"What's goin' on?" Jimmy asked, his head still twisted to look.

"Nothing. What's always going on? They're quiet people. I don't know what you're hoping to find."

"I mean with Rob." With his straddling, broad-shouldered walk, McSween nearly bumped Pearce as he came into the house. McSween was only a little man, five feet four if that, but Pearce seemed to spend a lot of time getting out of his way.

"Beer?" Pearce asked.

"Of course." They went into a kitchen so clean it seemed meals were never cooked in it.

"You know I'm worried." Pearce handed Jimmy a bottle and put water on to make himself a cup of tea.

"Have one yourself," Jimmy said.

"When are you going to stop telling me that?" Pearce said. "In ten more years? Have you ever seen me take a drink?"

Jimmy shrugged.

"You sound like you're giving me a tip," Pearce said. "If you're going to say that, why don't you leave a tip?"

"Habit," Jimmy said, spreading his elbows wide, making a triangle on the table top. He hunched over his drink.

"So what do you think about this Rocco?" Pearce asked.

"The first time I saw that kid in the gym —"

The bell rang in the hallway. "Christ, there's the boy."

When Jimmy nodded, Pearce was ready to do a double take, but he stopped and, surprising himself, looked at his friend with admiration. In spite of the way Jimmy talked and looked, with square face, big head, flat nose, two days' growth, and thinning brushcut, he was the guy who had really fought, he was the one who could, even as he seemed to stay in the background in the corner, calm fighters and sometimes, magically, get them to go beyond themselves. Not all the time, though.

"Get the boy a cup of tea, will you," Pearce said.

"Lemon," Jimmy said, and before Pearce could answer, "Just like after a workout."

He might talk to himself, Pearce thought, seem always a little off by himself, be matter-of-fact to the point of being oblivious, just out of it, but sometimes he was very shrewd. Nobody expected the things he picked up on, which was to Jimmy's advantage.

"You're a good man," Pearce said as he left, and meant it.

When Robbie and Pearce came back in together Jimmy said, "Hey, champ."

"What's up?" Robbie glanced around.

"Take your coat off," Pearce said. "Here's a tea."

Still standing in the doorway, Robbie took the mug and stared at the yellow wedge floating in it and said, "I ain't worked out."

"That's just what I said." Jimmy turned away.

"Relax," Pearce said.

Robbie sat down without taking his jacket off.

"So what's goin' on with this Roc?" Jimmy asked.

"What's going on," Robbie said. "What's going on? You were up there, you know what's going on. Nothing's going on! He didn't have to ask me. Anyway, he asked everybody. He didn't have to."

"Shiner's brought him in," Pearce said. "It's in your interests and our interests to know why, son."

"He's not Shine," Robbie said.

"He's a pal of Shiner's," Pearce said.

"He just asked me fishing," Rob insisted.

"Fishing," Pearce said. "Gimme a break."

"What's wrong with fishing?"

"Oh, come on, son."

"What are you talking about?" Robbie asked.

"Look," Pearce said. "You don't have a father."

"You knew my dad, didn't you, Stu," Robbie said.

"Yes, I did," Pearce said.

"What was he like?"

"One of the nicest guys in the world. How many times I told you?" Pearce said. "Don't you remember him?"

"Some things," Robbie said. "I remember grabbing his trouser leg one time when he asked me how I would feel about him going away on a trip, a long trip. All I could think of was that I would want him to come back."

"Yes," Pearce said gently.

"And he started you boxin'." Jimmy was upbeat, louder. "You said he started you in boxing."

"Not really," Rob said. "I mean, he invited another little kid in and I guess he'd bought boxing gloves and we'd tumble around the living room, but swinging. Yes," Rob said. "It was a kid I could take, his name was Chris Camalari, and I remember the furniture, rollin' up onto it almost."

"Well, that's good, eh," Jimmy said.

"I didn't like it much," Rob said.

"Oh, your dad was a good guy," Pearce said. "Remember how he had to put down his hat just right, he had to have it just right? A pearl grey fedora."

"No," Robbie said.

"I know your dad came in to the gym once," Jimmy said, "in a sharp suit, eh, with hundred-dollar bills pushed into his pockets. He must have made a killing."

"He was a customer's man," Pearce said. "No certificate. A guy that takes care of customers. At a stockbroking office. He wasn't a real stockbroker."

"We lived in a one-bedroom apartment," Robbie said.

"You watch the Friday-night fights with your dad?" Jimmy asked.

"Yes," Robbie said. "And I remember he liked Dick Tiger."

"Yes sir," Pearce said. "Yes sir. And you know your dad could talk to anybody. There wasn't a person he couldn't talk to. 'Go turn on the charm, Will,' your mum would tell him, 'turn on the charm.'"

"Uh-huh," Robbie said.

"And strong," Pearce said. "I seen him do a hundred pushups at a party — at a party! And I saw him stick out his chest and put two milk bottles on it."

With a soft smile that neither Pearce nor Jimmy had ever seen, Robbie said, "I used to walk around with my chest puffed out."

"You don't have to do that with the way you can hit," Jimmy said.

"No." Rob wasn't agreeing with Jimmy, he was thinking of something else. "I remember my dad," he said. "I know those stories."

"It's tough when you lose your dad so young," Pearce said.

"You know, he left me something," Rob said. "What I mean is, I found something of his the other day, it was a book he had, eh, a self-defence manual. Holds. It had in it instructions on how to pop an eye, get your thumb in and up and pop out an eyeball."

"Jesus!" said Pearce.

"That ain't boxin'," said Jimmy.

"No, I found it in my mom's room. It was Will's."

"Your dad was a lovely guy," Pearce said. "Everybody liked him."

They wound up not talking about Rocco, or Shiner, at least not in the way Pearce had intended. Jimmy did get at it, though, when he told Robbie about his own father. "I broke my arm and my old man was pissed off because I missed the provincials."

"Wow," Robbie said.

"I remember taking a terrific shot and him yelling from ringside, 'That didn't hurt!'"

"You guys aren't like that," Robbie had said.

What had Jimmy come up with then? "Get ready to be hated," he'd said into Robbie's face.

Rob was shocked. "Why?"

"'Cause you got talent," Jimmy said.

"Oh, come on," Pearce said. "Everybody won't let him down."

"Not you guys," Robbie had said.

That must have been what they wanted to hear, for Pearce, suddenly generous, blurted out, "That fishing wasn't much, but it was nice, eh? I mean, he didn't have to do that. You're right."

"It was nothing but great," Robbie said.

"Sure," Pearce said. "Boy, you're an intense kid."

"No, I'm not," Robbie said.

"No, he's not," Jimmy said.

"Well, people care about you," Pearce said. "You know that." It was a statement and a question.

"I guess so," Robbie said.

"Your mother doesn't want you to get hurt. Jimmy and I . . ."

"Sure," Rob said, and they'd left just after that.

Pearce was alone in the house with the kind of restless joy he seemed to have forgotten, a feeling like when he had been in training himself, and might have overtrained and couldn't sleep and had wandered around too late into the night. He was filled with optimistic possibilities and the hours went by.

Rob was safe. Whatever Rocco and Shiner were, they were a universe apart from that creep who had hung out at the club and wanted to "help with the boys" and had also wanted to be a lay brother and was interested in the military. All the danger signals going off at once and they had gotten rid of him fast. That was the kind of guy who lived with his mother people should worry about. Pearce felt angry people could ever, *ever* think of him with suspicion because he had never married and his life had become the gym and athletics; all those baseball teams he'd managed. What's wrong with that? It was a good, healthy life, outside in summer. And hell, most of them were women's teams; he'd met Katy on one of those teams for godsakes, the Wrigley's Chicklets.

It had taken him long, too long, to make his own life, but he had made it and with all the mistakes he was fine now.

That's when Stuart Ewell Pearce decided to wipe down, to disinfect the butcher's block in his kitchen. At two in the morning he mixed bleach and water, then passed his hand back and forth over wood that was hardly scratched. He ran the rag over all the countertops and tables, then the chairs. Stopping himself, alone, with that smell that reminded him of so much, he sat still in the bright lights until three o'clock in the morning.

Going upstairs at last, Pearce knew the Javex would smell on his hands when he got into his fresh cold bed, and that it would disappear as he closed his eyes and warmed up.

CHAPTER 8

"THIS IS ALL PIE IN THE SKY," Rocco didn't like the pain in his chest; he thought of that time deer hunting.

"You're right," Shiner said. "But you saw. There's something there."

"We're talking a thirteen-year-old boy here," Rocco said. Sunlight that was white at the glass doors of the Paddock Tavern, and the colour of beer where it reached the draft station and mixed with the light-bulbs above it, hurt his eyes. "Let's go downstairs to the bar if you want to drink."

"Sure." Shiner got up from the table, his left hand absently brushing below his belt. He's checking to see if his fly's unzipped, Rocco thought.

"You wonder how these places make money," Shiner said.

"They do all right." Rocco looked at the solitary men sitting in the room.

"How does the Rex do?"

"All right."

"Do you have to keep on top of the books? Get

robbed much? That's the restaurant business. Have to be on top of the thieves all the time."

"Yeah, well," Rocco said.

"I've got your cheque here." Shiner reached around to his back pocket; his suit coat opened as he twisted and his shirt bunched at the waist. Rocco had an urge to tell him his shirt tails were going to come out.

"Here you go," Shiner said.

"Thank you." As he took the money Rocco focused on the cheque, holding it close to his face, cheeks and nose getting rounder and his teeth showing wet and blue. Shiner wondered if he was grinning — a glinting, defiant, threatening grin — but saw it was a real smile.

"Is it okay?" Shiner asked.

"This is made out in the name of your trucking company, eh," Rocco said. "For services rendered."

"Well, it is a business expense," Shiner said.

Suddenly expansive, Rocco said, referring to bookmaking he did on the side, "Now this is not the easiest way in the world to make money."

"Hard to collect, eh?" Tucking in his shirt, Shiner nodded amiably.

So that's what's bothering me, Rocco thought. This guy always looks good; it's not right when he's a mess. "Anyone who makes money this way has earned it," he said.

"I'm going to be quiet for a while," Shiner said. "No more bets."

"That's the way," Rocco said. "Keep out of trouble."

"Just sure things."

"Tell me about them."

"This boy is as close to one as I've seen."

"You may be right," Rocco said. "But it's early, way too early."

"Let's go downstairs for a real drink."

They left the beverage room and went down to the emerald and black of the basement lounge; it was so dark the prints of racehorses on the wall could not be made out. Except for the barman there was no one else in the room.

"Grab a booth," Shiner said. "Want something to eat?"

"It's not lunch yet." What's with these English guys? Rocco wondered. He's having rye and water for breakfast, but it doesn't seem to affect him. It's like he just got up and shaved. Then he thought of Shiner's shirt coming out of his pants. "You putting on some weight?" he asked.

"I don't think so," Shiner said.

"Maybe you just don't like to pay your gambling debts," Rocco said.

"That's it. Who does? But I like to win."

"And you do."

They sat in a padded, circular booth. Rocco could hardly see his hands in front of him. "Gimme a coffee," Rocco called over. Shiner had another hard drink. "I gotta be going soon," Rocco said. "I'm going over to the hotel."

"Well, what do think about Robbie?" As he spoke Shiner reached for his drink, and knocked it over. Before Rocco could react Shiner pushed himself back so quickly that his body thudded against the vinyl behind him. The thump meant he'd hit wood. The spilled liquid had not yet reached the edge of the table.

"You okay?" Rocco asked.

"I have no idea."

Why, when people say that, is it always so aggressive? Rocco thought. "Relax," he said.

Shiner bent his head and, with both hands holding the table, stared down.

"It won't reach you," Rocco said.

"Yep." Shiner stood, and the barman came over and wiped up. "It wouldn't stain anyway," Shiner joked, then, "Well, what do you think about Robbie?"

"You're right, to a point," Rocco said. "From what I've seen he's something. But it's way too early. You have to wait and see if he keeps showing up. He might not. He might take time off, then come back to the gym. Why not? You're asking a lot."

"Not from what I've seen," Shiner said. "He loves it."

"You can ruin kids, eh," Rocco said.

"Pearce'll take care of that."

"Is that right. Pearce's good — for now."

"Want to come in on him?"

"Sure," Rocco said. "But slow down."

"You had us all up north fast enough."

"The kid looked like he needed it," Rocco said, though he knew that at the time of the invitation he hadn't been thinking that. "Christ, so do you. And Jimmy, Jimmy needs it permanent."

"Jimmy needs a rubber room," Shiner said.

"You think so?"

"Aw, he knows what he's doing, at least with Pearce around. Anyway, the thing is, the boy's a prodigy. He's way advanced. You can talk to anyone, you can ask anyone about it. Hell, you saw."

"In this game no one's a prodigy until they're fifteen, and that was in the bad old days."

"Put him in with some coconut-headed coon and he'll break his hands, eh," Shiner said.

"Sugar Ray Robinson was a prodigy and he wasn't really boxing until fifteen. And that's early."

"They got hard heads, those guys," Shiner said.

"What are you talkin' about?"

"No. Really. This goddam nigger wouldn't get out of one of my cabs —"

"Was he working for you?" Rocco asked.

"No!"

"So what was he doing in one of your trucks?"

"The point is, he wouldn't get out and I had to hit him in the head with a tire iron."

"Is that right."

"Didn't have no effect."

"You have to be careful."

"I'm serious. It didn't have no effect."

"Did he get out of the truck?"

Shiner grunted.

"So it had an effect."

They didn't speak for a while, Rocco glancing up to look at the reflections and points of light in the glasses hanging over the bar. His coffee was tepid. Neither of them smoked. "You have to be careful," he repeated.

"The guy I hit used to be a fighter." In letting Rocco know that, Shiner was making a definite point, which he immediately softened with a self-deprecating noise between a wheeze and a cough.

"That's all right."

"You might know him. He's been around boxing."

"Older guy?"

"Obnoxious. Stubborn bastard."

"Lame Crawford," Rocco said. "That's a guy took fits."

"I guess I didn't help," Shiner said.

◢

Out in the daylight again, Rocco thought about taking a run up north just by himself. At the Rex everything was fine — it could always be better — but after the meeting with Shiner he didn't want to be around any more beverage rooms during the day. Because the lake never took much more than an hour to get to, he could be back at the Rex that night by eleven, if he wanted, to get the money from a man named Motley — Frank Motley and his motley crew.

He decided against it; it was too much.

Shiner was a good client, but he had made Rocco restless. It wasn't that he owed any money, or that he was a rough guy; Rocco had dealt with guys a thousand times rougher. Yet being with him had made Rocco consider getting away.

I've got to forget it, he said to himself. What could Shiner do? He wasn't a lush, though he could drink, those English guys could drink. And he was a good customer, there was nothing wrong there. He was not dangerous. Rocco formed the words slowly, then quickly thought of guys who really were. But right away he thought of Shiner again and wondered if the guy was too sharp, too goddam clean.

It wasn't that Shiner would ruin the kid, but the way he'd tucked his shirt in like that, checking his fly — a thing like that in a well-dressed guy? Just for a second Shiner'd looked like a disaster.

Was it the boy, not the boy but Shiner's attitude to

him? Nothing wrong with wanting to cash in, and the kid really could punch, boy, he could punch.

Then Rocco thought of Jimmy's swollen face, remembered him at the lake talking about how swimming softened your muscles. "Boxing," Jimmy said. "Whoever made money in boxing?"

Rocco had.

And what could you tell this early?

Robbie Blackstone had looked like he could do with a little fishing. Did a young guy like that ever get a chance to fish? Rocco never had. Robbie obviously never got out of the city. Was it a question of his age? How old was he really?

Streetcars clanged through the intersection. Even a bright day like this, downtown, made him think of stone, glints in pebbles. And red brick looked too soft. He noticed paint flaking around the horsehead on the marquee above him. His eyes continued to bother him. Slowly, Rocco walked to his Lincoln.

CHAPTER 9

LOOKING UP through the chicken wire he had pushed away to get inside, Robbie saw high blue sky. Late afternoon in fall. The cupola of the Better Living Centre at the Canadian National Exhibition had never had anyone else in it; that's what it felt like in spite of the beer bottle by his foot. Robbie nudged the glass, the same amber as some of the leaves that covered the floor. The wood frame of the structure above him was black with mould and dust, but where he sat, now flexing his biceps and staring at the vein, was chilly-warm and strange — the leaves of his nest nearly all dry.

The climb, straddling a corner of the building and using thin ledges of brick for finger and toe holds, had been more difficult and dangerous than he'd thought, though when he finally reached the desert of tar-and-pebble roof he had started immediately for one of the domed, capped towers, going up again. At the top the grating against pigeons had been soft in his hands; he squeezed in and dropped down to be hidden above the world.

No one anywhere, and such a strange displaced feeling sitting hunched and quiet where he was.

The neighbourhood would be to his back, the bridge over the cut of the railway tracks that led to these grounds, his apartment building a way off, the streets and, just inside the Dufferin Gates, in the wind, the bench that he used to practise his trumpet. To the south was the flashing grey of the lake.

He could not go home now, the empty apartment would be so sparse, the light of a whole day having been trapped in it, overheated.

Here his face was oily from the outside, but he felt cosy, and cold; it was like he was not inside his body.

The library books on jazz, and his instrument, were hidden on the ground, by themselves, quiet without him.

The trumpet was over for him, not because of what Shine had said, but because he could not hit high notes, and he liked the books on jazz better than the music; it was the idea of the music that he read about, and the life, that he liked. The records he'd heard, the sound, were not connected in any way with what he had imagined. They didn't do at all what some songs did.

His embouchure was no good no matter how hard he worked, and right now his mouth hurt from sparring: thick lips thicker, the upper one swollen out — but it felt kind of nice. Staying after school with the band made him dizzy and tired.

On his way down here to practise he had seen, striding forcefully, crazily, over on the other side of the street, the professor. He was called "the professor," but not the way Shiner used the word when he called Pearce that. Big gut and goatee, big calves in shorts on a day like this, it was clear this professor was capable of shocking anger. But only if pushed, and the mocking of him never went too far. The professor even encouraged it, spluttering and puffing as he went along in that purposeful — always too busy — way of his, acknowledging "Professor!" But there was a threat in him. Robbie wondered if he lived in that half of a skinny house at the end of the street standing beside the hole of a new high-rise foundation. If he kept children in cages in the basement.

Thinking about it was scary, different from what he felt in boxing, nervous in a different way, more of having to go to the bathroom in it; he described it to himself as like from a fairy story, though he could not remember any fairy stories that Lucy had read to him when he was little. Empty, floating, detached from himself in the rustle of the leaves, Robbie thought of a child in a cage where the professor kept him.

◼

That night he went back to one of the first places he had learned to box. It meant a streetcar trip, and upsetting his mother, who said he should be doing his homework, but he had to go, knowing that the trip, the motion of the trolley and being by himself on it, the yellow lights and darkness of the city outside, would retain something of that hollowness he had felt earlier.

As would the dressing room of the Dovercourt Y, so dark at night, with the blinding tile of the shower stall down a corridor like a cave, dark green lockers, and the first time he had been there and going up to the gym or back down to the first floor and the ring.

Just a room, and a bag, not like with Pearce at Cabbagetown, but where he first saw he could do what he had done in Niagara Falls.

The other boy was dark and quick, a natural athlete, and he made fun of Robbie playing floor hockey. Made fun of him, and boxing, and because he was such a good athlete he challenged Rob.

The coach had warned the other boy — Rob did not even know his name — that Rob was a hard hitter. Rob wasn't sure what that meant. The comment, made as the boys were coming together, had no effect on the confident dance, the shock of hair and bright eyes in front of him, until Rob, hands up like he'd been taught, went forward and socked: straight, like he'd been taught. The surprise on the other guy's face was total.

Rob was himself surprised at the effect, but just a little. The punch was nothing, just solid — and he thought, So that's it, that's what they're talking about. Had he heard then what he had heard in Niagara Falls, and wondered if others could hear: a sound as when he had picked up the round, diseased body-ball of a baby pigeon under the bridge and dropped it a long way onto the cement?

Was the noise real when he connected? Wet and ugly, but matter-of-fact, what had to be done. Maybe he had not heard it at the Dovercourt Y.

There was the old man there who had once fought and wanted to go rounds with him after that, who banged his kidneys as they clinched, the first time anyone had done that: the guy's pink and splotchy and rough face and broken nose and watery eyes pressing up against him on the ropes. Rob's uppercut broke the dentures in his mouth and his eyes watered even more — was he crying? That stopped his shuffling and breathing on him. There were no more kidney punches. Where had the first, the good coach gone? The old guy with the saggy skin on his lower back and biceps took over and he didn't teach anything! He wasn't any coach — wheezing that boxing was the greatest sport in the world and putting his paws all over him. Rob'd knock him out now. He didn't go back much after that.

And afterwards, that first time, in the dressing room, so odd: wrapped in a towel, sitting on a bench in a big dark arched space where guys came up to talk to him; lights in shadows all around and wet on the floor and the night outside.

His dad had liked boxing. Rob remembered telling Pearce about watching the Friday-night fights with him, and him bringing home those smaller kids for him to fight, and Rob would overwhelm them, windmilling, both of them crying. There was the way it felt to be hit when you were a little kid.

Once he'd fought Jerry Shears in the alley and his dad had watched and not interfered and it had gone on too long and after it was over Robbie climbed the fire escape up to his father and grabbed his pant leg, just like he'd grabbed it when his dad asked him about going away. As he approached his father Robbie had begun to cry, and Will told him it was all right to cry then.

When Robbie got to the old Y that evening, all by himself, there was no one there. The room was the same but the place had changed. No boxing program, no people. After a look around he didn't even bother getting changed.

◤

Back at the apartment he found his mother in bed, sheets up to her chin, her head in the centre of the polished, nearly black headboard.

"Where have you been?" she asked.

"I've got to get my own room. My own bed."

"Where were you after school?"

"I went down to the Ex to practise. I'm going to sleep now."

"And tonight?"

"I went to the Y. It was a waste of time. Look —"

"What do you mean, your own bed? Ever since you were little you've had your own bed. I've had to sleep on the couch. You kicked like a mule."

"No, but, we share —"

"I couldn't afford anything after your father died! Do you know what this apartment costs a month?"

"What about Shiner? If another apartment comes available in the building can we get it? A two-bedroom. 708."

"Who'll pay for it?"

"Can't you ask Shiner to help?"

"Here, go to bed." Abruptly she got out and turned back the covers. In her bare feet, and with her nightgown slightly billowing, she seemed much smaller than he was. Her face was puffy and pale, but not from anger any more. "I'm tired," she said.

"That's okay," Rob said. "I think I'll have a bath."

"Oh, take it," she said. "Don't come into the living room. I'll be asleep."

In the middle of the night the door to the bedroom opened. A fan of illumination entered the room. Was it his mother? Something wrong? But Lucy was back and curled up far away from him on the other side of the mattress. She'd gotten uncomfortable on the couch. Rob rolled even farther to his side, as far away from her as he could, realizing he'd sensed a shock, but closing his eyes to go back to sleep.

Shiner was below them, at the foot of the bed. Like a gate, the crossbeam of the bedposts stretched in front of his crotch. He gave a clear impression he'd stopped and wasn't going to move farther forward for a moment. Feet braced, Shiner stood tall.

Thinking the lights should go on, Rob saw his mother was awake. Nothing happened. With a grin as if he'd just shoved a cigar in the side of his mouth to get it out of the way and was about to impatiently demonstrate the right way to do something — Rob expected to hear "Gimme that!" — Shiner just grinned some more.

Was the smell alcohol or aftershave?

"I'll show ya a leg lock, little girl," he said. "I saw the Whipper tonight. How 'bout a toe hold?"

"You're drunk," Robbie said.

"C'mere." Shiner bent forward and grabbed playfully at Lucy as if she was a little animal under the covers.

"Stop it!"

So loud. She was right to say no but she was too loud. "Mum," Robbie said.

"C'mere!" Bent over the bedpost, Shiner rested on one fist and grabbed.

"Don't." Lucy curled into Robbie. Her son wasn't sure if she needed help or was protecting him.

"Don't," he said.

"Ahhhh." Lucy was louder still. Shiner had not touched her.

"Don't," Robbie said.

Now he caught her leg, which came out the side from under the bedspread. Twisted it around his arm — leg and arm were like two snakes. Biting his lower lip, concentrating, Shiner said "Eh," like a question. "Eh?"

"Hey," Robbie said.

Instantly Shiner let her go, went back to his full height over them, and swelled his chest.

"He'll kill us. He'll kill us." Lucy was pressed against Robbie, half clutching him, half pushing him away. "He'll kill us."

CHAPTER *10*

"I LIKE A CLEAN HEAD." With a broad, expansive gesture Shiner ran his whole hand over his brushcut. Up to his knees in the lake, he stumbled on uneven footing.

Rocco watched from the dock. It was late spring. Mayflies over the water and some of the trees still flowering; the filigree, the lime green of new leaves making a corridor above the beach road.

Oblivious of Rocco, but not talking to Lucy either, who treaded the slate and shiny water, or to Robbie, who stood fully dressed on the cobbles by the shore, Shiner said, "My grandfather would say, 'What good is that long hair on those young guys? Keep a clean head.'" His voice was so hoarse and confiding it was almost a whisper.

"You talking to yourself?" Rocco called over but he didn't get a response as Shiner stumbled again. His boxer trunks were so low that his stomach with its big navel stuck out like an infant's; the crack of his buttocks was not quite visible.

Rocco turned his head away from the glistening,

hairless body, only the forearms and hands freckled with colour, and the neck.

Shiner fell completely and sat in the water up to his waist. His skin was alabaster, flawless, but too smooth, too tight.

"Christ," Rocco mouthed.

Shiner laughed. "What's that?"

"Want another drink?"

Without answering, Shiner rolled over, lying face down. He began to move his arms like flippers against the lakebed and pushed out towards Lucy.

"You going in?" Rocco called over to Robbie.

"Not now."

"Where's Pearce and the J?" he asked.

"They've gone to town," Robbie said. "Then they're going to a drive-in."

"On a date?" Rocco said. "Every time I have those two clowns up here they're never here. The first time I invited them they hardly showed. They never fish, they never swim. I don't think either of them ever had his clothes off outside a gym. Hell, I don't think Pearce ever had his clothes off. What do they really do?"

"They go to town," Robbie said. "Then they're going to the drive-in. And they'll be home late."

"They told you that?"

"Yep."

"I'll leave the door open," Rocco said, looking back out to the lake.

Shiner was floating now and he began to swim. He lifted his head and called to Lucy with an exaggerated parody of obedience, "I'm com-ing."

"Sh-ine," she matched his tone and sidestroked in his direction.

"Cornball," Rocco said under his breath. The whole performance was designed to exclude everybody else.

Soon they were facing each other, bodies ghostly beneath the surface.

"Hey." Shiner grinned.

Robbie watched it all.

"Come on up to the house," Rocco said to him.

Lucy's face was puffy because of her tight bathing cap; her lipstick was heavy but faded to coral in the centre.

Eyes wide, Lucy moved closer than it seemed Shiner expected. He kept smiling at her, smiling and smiling, but now his stare was fixed, as if he was trying to look through and past her.

Rocco wondered whether she was saying anything: her mouth was mobile, then drawn and full. Whatever she was saying was assuring, as to a reluctant, even a cornered, child. On she came.

Shiner's demeanour changed. He glanced quickly to both sides. It wasn't fun any more.

"Ohoooo." Delighted, and continuing to play and reassure him, she got closer.

"Let's go," Rocco said to Robbie.

Was she aware of the noise she was making? Robbie stood silent.

Was it saliva or lake water making Lucy's smile so wet? Whatever she was feeling was going to be shared, that was clear.

Now she was in his arms. They started to go down. "Heh," Shiner laughed at the sky, relaxing again, not looking at her, his neck swelling as he arched backward.

They went under, and Rocco could make out her

limbs around Shiner's body, but not his arms or legs. "Come on up to the house," he said to Robbie.

They surfaced.

"Hmmmmmm." Lucy's noise, though slightly oblivious of Shiner, was the equivalent of it's okay, we're having a fun ride. But she was locked on him and he was having trouble holding them both up.

"I gotta swim." He broke free.

"You comin' or what?" Rocco rolled sideways and prepared to push himself up, about to dutifully joke about having short arms and being stiff, when he saw that Robbie had disappeared.

◥

"A fat drunk," Shiner said.

"Will used to know him," Lucy said. "We'd see him at Davisville and he'd say to me, 'That's Tom Longboat.' But I didn't pay much attention."

"Didn't you know who he was, Mum?" Robbie said.

"Will could talk to anybody."

"He had the gift of the gab, eh?" Rocco said.

"But did you know who he was?"

"A fat drunk," Shiner insisted.

"Will said something about him running. I didn't pay much attention."

"What was he like?" Robbie asked.

"A fat drunk." Shiner used the exact staccato he had the first time.

"Come on," Rocco said irritably, and he leaned forward gently on the card table. After supper, the cottage felt much quieter than usual. It was dark, depthless, beyond the windows. Pearce and Jimmy had not shown up, and Shiner, Rocco, Robbie, and

Lucy sat under a light in the kitchen. "He was a great runner," Rocco said. "You must know that."

"A fat drunk." Though Shiner shrugged with some kind of concession.

With a challenge in his voice, Rocco said, "He was a big Onondaga."

"A what!"

"An Onondaga." Rocco nodded. "Uh-huh," anticipating Shiner's response, mocking him but with some approval, friendly.

"An Onondaga. What's that? A nigger?"

"An Indian. An Onondaga. From Brantford."

"Yeah, a fat drunk!"

"You get your teeth capped, or what?" Rocco snapped, jerking his head forward to stare at Shiner's jaw.

Shiner closed his mouth and looked at Lucy. "Dr. Watinski?" He paused. "He owed me some money and that's how he paid me."

"It took a week," Lucy said. "You were never in more pain in your life."

"I don't remember saying that."

"You were in that chair for a week."

Shiner grunted. "Well, I can't take 'em out and put them in a glass for you," he said to Rocco.

"No, no," Rocco said, as quickly conciliatory as he had been angry. "Everybody's got a bridge or something." Almost summer, and the night shouldn't have been like this, he thought. If you stepped outside you wouldn't see anything. In spite of everything, he was glad he had asked them to visit, and Robbie was an appreciative kid. When a day like today was over, the house would have seemed so empty and his wife was away.

"Do you two want to play checkers?" Lucy asked. "Shine and I can go for a walk." A kerchief was wrapped around her head like a turban, but she had tied it so that two ears of cloth stood up at each corner. She wore trousers, more like ski slacks because they tapered and had a strap across the bottom, and gold slippers. The crescent of skin that showed of her feet was very white. "It's damp," she said.

Rocco stared past the curtains to the pane of silver and black glass that was closest to him. "Is it raining? I don't like soft rain. If it rains it should rain. I like to hear it come down."

"You're not hot in that sweater?" Shiner asked Lucy.

"It's cotton."

"You like to run?" Rocco turned to Robbie. "How do you know about Tom Longboat?"

"Stu told me about him."

"He was before Stu's time," Rocco said.

"Really?" Robbie said.

"You runnin' up here?" Shiner asked Robbie. "You get up in the morning and go out?"

"Who likes roadwork?" Rocco answered, though he made a general gesture by lifting his arms off the table, palms up.

"There's no traffic. It's great up here," Shiner said.

"Do *you* go out?" Rocco asked him.

"Yeah." Shiner's sarcasm was distracted; he looked across the room with empty, blue eyes. "To the car."

"I run," Robbie said. "It's the foundation."

"Stu tell you that?" Rocco said, then before Robbie could answer, "Fighters like to fight, though."

"I don't run too far," Robbie said.

"Well, Pearce is right," Rocco said. "It's the base."

"He's too young to run too far," Lucy said. "He's growing. His bones."

"That's ending," Shiner said.

"What, he's not growing?" Rocco said.

"I go a couple of miles," Robbie said. "It's good."

"I can't believe it's two years since I met you," Rocco said, crinkling the skin by his temples, his wide thin mouth getting wider, sharpening into a scythe below his round cheeks and his wide, flattened nose. This sense of a shared, funny secret, his charm, was not always sincere; it usually had the effect he wanted it to, however. Right now he was surprised at what he felt. "You're doin' fine," he said, and meant it.

"Nearly three," Lucy said.

"What's that?"

"Nearly three years," Lucy said.

"He's growing up," Rocco said.

"Not really," she said.

"It is time to get serious now," Rocco said. "I mean, boxing takes a lot of dedication. If you're serious it can become your whole life: your mother, and your father." Rocco looked right at Rob. "Your whole life."

"Nothing is ever as important as a mother," Lucy said. "I read . . . I mean, it's natural. There is no greater bond than mother and child."

"I'm not a child," Robbie said.

"I'll tell you what boxing can mean," Rocco said. "Down in the States, the Southern States, when they brought in a new way of executing prisoners, capital punishment —"

"Hang the bas'ards," Shiner said.

"That's just what I'm getting to," Rocco said. "They

stopped hanging the — bastards by the way, not 'bas'ard.'"

"Murdering bastards," Shiner said.

"Oh, Shine," Lucy said.

"They stopped hanging the poor bastards and decided to gas them. Poison gas took over. It was the new thing."

"The gas chamber," Robbie said.

"That's right. And the so-called scientists, the scientific observers, put a microphone in there to hear the words of the dying prisoner. The first victim was a young negro, and as the gas came in you know what he said? You know what the guy said?"

"There you go with the niggers," Shiner said. "There ain't no niggers around here."

"Well, there's niggers in boxin'," Rocco sneered. "In case you hadn't noticed."

"What did he say?" Lucy asked, then added, "Shoot 'em all, that's what my mother used to say, shoot 'em all."

"She was talking about the French-Canadians, Mum," Robbie said.

"I know," Lucy said.

"The guy said —" Rocco paused, "'Save me.'"

"Wasn't nobody going to save him then," Shiner snorted.

"No, no," Rocco said. "He said, 'Save me. Save me, Joe Louis.'"

"So?" Shiner said.

"Save me, Joe Louis." Rocco shook his head in amazement. "I understand."

"Did you ever see Joe Louis fight?" Robbie asked.

"Yes, I did."

"Against Marciano? You see him against Marciano?" Shiner said, the challenge in his voice meant to mirror what had happened to Joe Louis.

"No, I didn't see that fight," Rocco said. "But I saw a Joe Louis fight, and I saw Joe Louis. Joe Louis was a dignified man."

"I'm going to bed," Shiner said, and pushed his chair back.

"I don't ever want Robbie to have as many fights as Joe Louis," Lucy said. "He was from the Depression, my God."

"That's the way it should be," Rocco said. "That's how you should think. It's all going to pick up soon enough for Rob, believe me. You don't want him to have no two hundred fights — I think that's what Joe Louis had, including exhibitions. Can you imagine? Over two hundred fights, for a heavyweight. You don't want that to happen, and it won't. There's a lot of people in our boy's corner. And Pearce is smart, in his way."

"I'm surprised my son hasn't lost interest." Lucy wiggled a little on her seat, to draw the attention back to herself.

"Oh, Robbie hasn't lost interest," Shiner said. He was sitting away from the table, but hadn't made a move to leave.

"How many fights have you had, Robbie?" Rocco asked.

"I'm not sure."

"You don't count that first one, the first time I saw you, as a fight, do you?"

"I'm not sure," Robbie said again.

"I'm kidding ya," Rocco said.

"I think I better go to bed," Robbie said.

"You never go to bed this early," Lucy said.

"There's nothing to do."

"You have to get up early, eh?" Rocco said.

"We should go back tomorrow," Shiner said.

"You're not staying the weekend?"

"The weather, you know," Shiner grimaced, as if bravely accepting bad news beyond his control. Then he got up, and left.

It was after midnight, and Pearce and Jimmy had not returned from town. Rocco lay awake, worrying about leaving the door unlocked, even up here. As he'd gotten older, he'd always been able to go right to sleep. But not tonight.

This was an expensive cottage, but now the walls seemed thin, paperboard. Was it birds, or rain — scuffles and ticking outside in the dark? Did it have to do with the damp?

On the cot in the partitioned-off closet that served as his bedroom Robbie was also awake. But he had come out of sleep because he had heard something. There was only a curtain between him and the hallway.

There it was, a disembodied voice, crying to heaven, not expecting an answer, but having to cry. "I can't help it; I love you."

On the edge of weeping, so full of grief it seemed reckless of being heard, the noise was part of the dim quiet, but was also clear, alive.

Grief was when someone died, Robbie thought. Nobody had died.

In Robbie's cubicle the light under the draped

cloth that served as a wall was a rich rose. He was alarmed, and got up.

As Robbie pushed the folds of the curtain back, he knew the sound was from his mother, but he didn't want to think it was.

Rocco heard it too, and the sounds of feet, the creaking of wooden floors. It made him get out of bed.

Both Robbie and Rocco looked out into the passageway, neither of them quite sure what this watching would do but feeling they had to do something.

They saw him together, first his bulk in the shadow down by the open bathroom door, then Shiner stepped out into the bright light. He was naked.

The glow framed his length, his gleaming stomach and reddish pubic hair.

There was such a lack of self-consciousness on Shiner's part that at first Rob thought it was okay.

Then he didn't like it at all.

Ah, the kid shouldn't have to see that, Rocco said to himself.

With his very casualness, Shiner seemed to be making too big a thing about being nude.

The same words, a throat half swallowing them, "I can't help it; I love you. I love you," came from behind a door. All three men attended, but it caused a small physical change in Shiner, a shiver. Then he was completely still again, illuminated, lost in his thought, but surly now, with a pouting, self-obsessed, nearly absolute indifference.

From out of the darkness down there the noise went on, and Robbie knew he shouldn't have to hear it.

Then there was a thump outside. Everyone paid attention. The words stopped.

Rocco stepped forward, he had thrown on the clean plaid shirt that he fished in, and underpants. In spite of his shirt Rocco felt cold, though it was a warm, greasy night.

With one hand clenched on his breast, Rocco felt a pain that was different from anything that he had felt when he was fighting, or doing what he'd had to do for a living, or even when his chest had cramped when he was alone in the woods.

There was a louder thump, then a bang. No lights went on, but suddenly Pearce and Jimmy were bumping down the hall. They ran into each other again.

"For God's sake," Pearce said.

"By the sweet jumpin' Jesus, would you look at that," Jimmy said when he saw Shiner.

Taking an unhurried step, Shiner moved sideways, then firmly shut the bathroom door.

Robbie dropped back into his cubicle; Rocco into his own room. Pearce and Jimmy stood there. The central passageway was as dim and hushed as if it was the middle of the night and everyone had been asleep.

"Put your goddam clothes on," Jimmy whispered to no one in particular.

CHAPTER **11**

THE NEXT MORNING Pearce watched Rocco come across the lawn towards him. Why did they describe someone who was built like that as a fireplug? That sounded too much like spark plug. It was fire hydrant they meant, built like a fire hydrant. Though he was wearing a bulky robe and carrying a big towel over his shoulder, the shape of Rocco's body was certainly distinctive. At this distance, with his still dark hair and bulbous, wide nose, the knotted skin of Rocco's forehead looked almost warty. Pearce wiped his own smooth brow. That must be scar tissue, he thought, and decided to look for little white triangles in Rocco's brow ridges when they talked.

"Mr. Rocco," Pearce said elaborately, but with a great deal of good nature in it.

Drying his hair, Rocco looked up at him. "Where's trainer number two?"

"I'd say he was hung, sir, yes, definitely hung, and is enjoying the pleasures of his solitary bed."

"Yeah."

"At least he refused to come when I called him." Instead of meeting Rocco's glance, Pearce looked down, to the grass, to Rocco's slick, yellow shins coming out of all that cloth and leading into leather bedroom slippers. In spite of wearing what Pearce thought of as enough towelling to supply a sauna, the hair was still plastered to Rocco's legs.

"I never thought I'd hear it from you," Rocco said. "Not from you."

"What? You don't think the lad's ready?" Pearce said. "You must have started on a professional career that young."

Surprise, disappointment, a look that said Pearce should have known better, all combined in a faint, general disgust that showed in the way Rocco shook his head. "Not yet sixteen," he said. "And it's a different world now."

"I don't mean right away, of course," Pearce said.

"Is it you, you and Jimmy, who think he's ready? You know the boy. Or is it Mum and Dad?"

"To be honest, sir, I am ambivalent," Pearce said. "On the one hand he is supremely talented, on the other he is a child."

"You some kind of Irish?" Rocco asked.

"Pardon?"

"You sound Irish, talking like that," Rocco said. The ingratiation had passed a boundary, Rocco felt. Kidding could get so darn close to insults. This with the boy was serious.

"Not at all," Pearce said, and in a different tone of voice. "I'm not trying to sell you on anything. I sincerely want to know what you feel."

"Well, he's too goddam young," Rocco said. "And

what about the Olympics and all that? Or the amateurs here?"

"You mean a national championship. That can happen, that will happen."

"Are you so sure?"

"You've seen him," Pearce said. "I've never seen anything like him all the years I've worked with kids."

"And that's it," Rocco said. "He's a kid."

"I'll tell you something," Pearce said. "And I truly believe this, I've thought about it a lot. You see, I wonder what all those punches you take in the amateurs, and you do take them, headgear or not — that mainly stops the cuts. Well, I wonder about the effect."

"And he'll be treated more gently as a pro?"

"Not at all," Pearce said. "It's the number of overall rounds in a career that concerns me. With three hundred amateur fights under your belt and then turning pro? You've been around the track as much as someone who starts early professionally. Isn't it better to reach your goal relatively fresh and get out?"

"And most of the guys get out at the right time, eh?"

"Okay, I'm not saying that. But there is pressure here, and I wanted to talk to you about the long-term *focus*. Is a long amateur career the way to go?"

"Who have you been talking to about this?"

"I wanted to talk to you."

"Have you talked to his mother?"

"I have. You know, there is no denying the word is out on Robbie, and not just in Toronto."

"I know who you been talking to and that's Shiner."

"Certainly, but you see —"

"And that's a man what drinks too much."

"Irish?" Pearce tried to joke.

"Have you seen his liver?"

"His liver?"

"His liver. You can see it through his shirt. Look at him in a golf shirt, you can see the bulge of it stand out from his body like a long fat leech."

"He holds his liquor," Pearce said.

"Think what a liver shot would do to him." Rocco narrowed his eyes, looked almost slyly at Pearce. When Pearce didn't respond Rocco said, "So you want to make a lot of money on him right away."

"That's not true at all. What money will I make?"

"You're listening to Shiner."

"Yes. Through his mother, I imagine, if that's what you imply. And I'd like to listen to you."

"Well, the *focus* is, he's too young," Rocco said with finality. "In his head." Then he softened. "You're thinking of someone like Sugar Ray, eh. The Harlem Fancy Dan. Club fights at sixteen."

"Robbie's phenomenal," Pearce said. "He truly is. I'm not saying he's like Sugar Ray Robinson." He smiled at Rocco, trying to share mutual knowledge and memories. "But he is phenomenal. And Sugar Ray filled Madison Square Garden when he was seventeen years old. His pro debut."

"Is that what you're thinking of?"

"It's certainly possible," Pearce said. "It could be, something like that. But here. On a smaller scale, maybe, smaller numbers. And as I said, in fast, out fast."

"You think he'll get out?"

"You did."

Rocco grunted. "Does Rob even want to go the pro route? It would have to be against the law to start him now. He's a Canadian kid."

"But I'm not talking *right now*," Pearce said.

"Well, who knows," Rocco said.

"It's wonderful the way you have the boy and his family up here," Pearce said.

"What are ya gonna do?" There was a pause. "Anyway, Shine and the Luce took off this morning. You guys are babysitting now."

Pearce nodded. He was dressed in yesterday's clothes, grey flannels and a white shirt. He looked uncomfortable.

"Don't you have summer stuff?" Rocco asked, then smiled broadly as he changed the subject. "He has it, Robbie has it. But don't you go listening to no Shiner."

"He's his guardian."

"Is he? Is he his legal guardian? They aren't married."

"I wouldn't know."

"Oh, you know. Do you think a guy that drinks like that knows what he's doing?"

"He seems to do quite well," Pearce said.

"Yeah?"

"I mean in terms of business."

"If he's so rich why ain't he smart, right?"

"Pardon?"

"If you're so smart why ain't you rich?"

"Mr. Rocco . . ."

"The thing, in this game, is to last. Above all, to last."

"Fighters can go on too long," Pearce said.

"It would be good if he could get out at the right time," Rocco said. "You create a miracle and get him out at the right time. But you might not be the right trainer for him when he's pro. Has Shiner told you that?"

"We have you," Pearce said.

"I'm no trainer," Rocco said. He could see Pearce was hurt, the taller man had drawn back as if struck.

"Rob has good defensive skills." Pursing his mouth, and tucking his chin primly in, Pearce took credit for them.

"That's right," Rocco said.

"They are completely important," Pearce emphasized.

"How far do you think the classic open stance, the stand-up pop-pop amateur posture, will take him as a pro?"

"So help out," Pearce said.

"He's beyond that style already," Rocco admitted.

CHAPTER *12*

THE LANDSCAPE FELL AWAY to his left, dark and flat, out to the pale sheet of the lake.

"That's cedar," Pearce said to Robbie, thinking, as he turned the wheel, of what Rocco had said when he had insisted they take his car — "Don't be such an old woman."

The hesitation Pearce had expressed was politeness, a way to show gratitude! Couldn't Rocco respond to that? I guess I showed it too eagerly, Pearce thought, dwelling on how the tone of what Rocco said was unlike the way Jimmy said the same thing in the gym, yelled it out, even. But Jimmy's comments seemed to be general; they were about Jimmy and his own state of mind.

Dismissing other people, that's what it was, Pearce thought. When Robbie had jogged in after his road-work and Rocco called to him, Pearce felt he'd ceased being present. A wave of tiredness, general fatigue, overcame him; he felt pallid, as if he had never been out in the sun. Living in a city, driving too much in the country; there never was any summer in Canada.

How similar were Rocco and Shiner? This big, black boat of a car was the equivalent of a cabin cruiser, the kind of boat Shiner owned, but Pearce couldn't help liking the ride. It was what his mother would have called a roadster. And Rocco had been so open-handed about letting them take it, though curiously insisting that Pearce drive Robbie to Martyrs' Shrine.

Was it some kind of Catholic thing to have them visit there? Rocco said it wasn't, he hadn't even been to Midland himself. Had he simply wanted to impress them with his car? The smooth quiet inside, without the radio going, both comforted Pearce and made him uneasy. "Does a big job like this make you nervous?" he asked Robbie, grinning.

"No."

"It's so damn easy to handle," Pearce said.

"You drive really well, Stu."

"That's a hell of a flood plain down there," Pearce said. "Even with this elevation you can see a long way. We'll drive all day just below the Shield. You'd never see that on the Canadian Shield."

The sky was huge and hazy, the colour of the far water. It seemed to him that every time he had driven north and come to where the rock started, the sky changed. Did it have something to do with being forced closer to the earth, surrounded even, going through rock cuts? It was not that simple. Was it the absence of sedimentary rock? It certainly wasn't distance; you could also see forever from moderate elevations in the North.

"How come you know so much?" Rob asked, but

he said it without the resentment Pearce had often faced whenever he talked about what he knew. I must not be bitter today, he said to himself, as one of his earliest memories welled up. "Little Stu has such a great fund of general knowledge." A man of sixty and he could remember it, said with such triumphant superiority, fully, smugly convinced such knowledge wouldn't do any good.

Did Rocco resent something like that in him, because he obviously knew about Martyrs' Shrine? "So take the kid," he'd cut Pearce off. Why the hell should Rocco get angry if someone knew something? Lots of reasons, lots, and he would not make a litany of them. Enjoy this day.

"Do I bore you with this stuff?" Pearce asked.

"I just want to know," Robbie said neutrally.

"It'll be a long drive." Was he trying to punish Robbie, telling him that? Rocco kicked him so he kicks Rob? Lord.

When Rob didn't respond Pearce said, "I only ask because there's a lot to see."

"That's okay."

"Rob," he deliberately said the boy's name.

"Yeah?"

"It's a bit longer but we'll go around the east side of the lake."

"Whatever."

"There are some good things this way."

"That's great."

"The Narrows at Lake Couchiching are a hell of an ancient place. The Indians used it for thousands of years as a special fishing spot. Champlain remarked on it."

"Is it still good fishing?"

"Sure, has to be."

"How do you know all this?" Rob kept on it.

"You mad at me because I know?"

"No." Now he was irritated.

I better stop, Pearce thought. Whatever had gone on — and Pearce thought there had been a sliver of justification in his sensitivity to Rocco — Rob liked him. But Pearce couldn't leave it alone. "Is there something wrong with me because I'm interested in things?"

Rob considered. "I'm not saying there's something wrong wit' you."

"You mean *with* me."

"Whatever." Then he said each word like a separate sentence. "I — just — wondered — how — you — knew — so — much."

Pearce admitted, "I've been thinking of something else," then, briskly, "Did you ever get the Shrine in school?" And before Rob had a chance to speak, "We didn't. In my day."

"Not really." Rob considered. "We had Quebec, in a way. Sort of in civics."

"Civics! Look, when I was a kid, today even, the only place you could find out about Martyrs' Shrine and some of what went on was in Catholic pamphlets. Catholic books about the Jesuit martyrs, really. It's an incredible story but all you can get is the one side. I mean, they came up through Toronto."

"Who did?"

"The Iroquois."

"Through Toronto." Rob wrinkled his forehead.

"Can't believe it?" Pearce said. "That mean it

doesn't matter? Well, you have the right attitude, the general attitude."

"No, but . . ."

"It's okay," Pearce said quickly, with good humour. "Look, there isn't a good general history. But you ask how I know? As a kid when I first heard, then read, about these things — I think it was a mention in class, or a friend of my mother's — it was as if this incredible thing had happened, then disappeared, or nearly. And right here. Nobody knew about it, or was interested, I guess. And whatever myth had developed, in holy cards or what some people, it seems not a lot of people, believed, didn't seem connected to what must have gone on. And it did go on." Elation came over Pearce; he felt he was telling the truth about a certain kind of indifference that, however tough it might be, was not hopeless. The thing itself was there. He suspected his mood swing, but smiled broadly at Rob.

"But there's a big church there, Mr. Rocco said."

"Yes, and we'll see it. But it's the sense of things I'm talking about, the sense anything ever happened in Canada. Look around."

"Yeah."

"It doesn't feel it. We've done something to this landscape. It doesn't feel anything happened here. Yet the depth of time is, the place, the wonder is —"

"But *you* know about it."

"We are going to see," Pearce said adamantly.

There was haze over undulations in the highway, which stretched ahead, and the inland feel of the road made it not seem to matter that the great lake was out of sight, off to their left. Brightness remained inside the light, but it got a little greyer; an excess humidity.

This seems to be the climate of my life, Pearce thought. But it's not the country's fault. Around here, what was done, what people built, how they saw the land, the place, how I see — can see — it, all missed something. "We have to take a look," he said.

"I'm interested." Rob made the veins in his forearm swell and looked at them.

He's a teenager, Pearce thought.

◤

After forty-five minutes they turned east, and when they approached Lake Couchiching, Pearce, still enthused, saw through the trees what he felt he had been looking for. "Look at that," he said.

"It's an island."

"Look at it, it's different," he insisted, and it was. The landscape had changed. There were three dark islands, not cedar, but dark on the lake, with the water around them. They seemed to clear the very air, Pearce thought, they're archaic.

"Look at that," he said again.

"Are there cottages on them?" Rob asked.

"Even if there are, do you get a feeling from them?"

"It's different, not so many houses," Rob said.

"Well, we may have turned Southern Ontario into a prairie, but there is something very old in those islands. Canada is very old."

"Like reindeer horns," Rob said.

"No reindeer around here," Pearce said. "Never were. But I think that's what I mean."

Then they saw the bridge, a swell in the pavement before them; some houses and a peeling square structure that abutted the shoulders.

"Let's stop," Pearce said, and nodded. "That's a tavern. Want a beer?"

Rob didn't smile.

They walked up the rise of the bridge single file, Pearce in his windbreaker not much taller than Rob. There was no sidewalk. At the height of the arch they stopped. Cars passed close behind them. Below the water ran dark and green, some of it with long streaks of pollen on the surface, some with grey dust. To the south was a point with a cedar leaning out over a patch of dark, unmarked, beige sand.

"There's obviously a current," Pearce said as he stared along the west shoreline.

It was bare rock. Granite and concrete powder covered everything, including the rubber tires of the blasting shields, the idle heavy equipment, and still water in small bays.

"They're building a marina." Rob read a toppled sign. "Is this the narrows?" He leaned over as if to see below the surface and find fish.

"Completely denuded," Pearce said. "There were weirs. The foundations, traces, might still be underwater. That would have meant huge catches, like commercial fishermen." And before Rob could answer, or Pearce could think about it and analyze the fishing techniques of long-dead Indians who needed to feed their families, he blurted out, "Any other place in the goddam world would have a plaque. Look at it."

"They're building a marina," Rob said.

◢

The church rose up before them from a dip in the highway, two-spired, with a thin wrought-iron cross between, the bottom of its facade hidden by the yellow-green shoulder of the hill. Behind the spires was blue sky.

From where they had turned south of Waubaushene, past Victoria Harbour and Port McNicoll, they had caught glimpses of the bay. Perhaps because the land was rolling, or the body of water so vast, the soft pastel light of the day opened up, became big.

"There used to be boat trains out of Port McNicoll," Pearce said. "My grandmother took thcm. You'd never know, eh. Gone."

"What's Waubaushene mean?" Rob had asked.

"I don't know," Pearce said.

"My dad used to say that if you got a new word and used it three times a day you had it for life."

"I don't think I could use Waubaushene three times a day," Pearce said. "Coldwater, yes, I could use coldwater. We used to have to put kettles of hot water in the bath when I was little to heat it up. How good that curl of heat would feel."

"My mother takes a lot of baths," Rob said.

"Well, it can relax you."

They drove through planted pine woods that came close to the car. Then, soon, they were there.

"Let's pull the car over here," Pearce said, slowing abruptly, the wheels making a strangely loud sound on the gravel.

"What?" Rob seemed alarmed, the steady quiet that had cocooned him for two hours suddenly smashed, first by the tires crunching stone, now by silence.

"This is it," Pearce said.

"But the church is . . ."

"Over there." Pearce nodded to a low triangular stone wall in a field corner; a rail, rusted wire, fence posts.

They walked down through a ditch, then up into the edge of brown pasture. Grasshoppers flew and brushed on their pants.

"Here we are," Pearce said.

Rob stood on some creaking squares of wire. The fence didn't run very far.

Other stones than the ones piled near them, these darker, more of them square and broken, lay on the surface of the earth. There were only a few, but there was a sense, a strong sense, that they had been put there. Rob and Pearce both felt a small, joyous sense of surprise, and they both had the sense of, if not an outline, at least the direction of the ruin.

"That's the foundation of the old fort?"

"Yes, it is."

The boy climbed the fence and walked around. He left Pearce behind him, and went out a little distance. Does he seem younger than he is? Pearce wondered. No. Rob looked at the ground, and Pearce thought, he's walking through a field of light.

CHAPTER *13*

THE IMPLEMENTS, crutches mainly, but artificial limbs, remembrance cards and relics, rosaries, canes, looked like they had grown out of the wall. It was dark. In the greenish vestibule with open doors Pearce stood talking to the priest. Inside, where Rob stood, was the interior of the church: tall, dim, some wood, shadows as grey as rain clouds, except for the very bright stained glass of martyrs in modern cassocks standing in harmless flames while a native, dressed a little like a Plains Indian, raised his arm.

Though the clutter in front of him was hard, it seemed to Rob organic, and he thought of images he couldn't name — molluscs accreting on each other, lichen on a rock. Though the display looked varnished, Rob realized it was simply the inertia of the implements: fossilized growths. His stomach was hollow. He had that feeling of being alone, that hollow feeling he sometimes had when he thought of the professor. Did the wire and wood before him make him think of a cage? The feeling was deeper than that, the feeling he had when he didn't even seem to be there: the motion, the current, the bass note inside. He thought of death.

◢

The first apartment was important, two-storey, and as you went in the door there was a bathroom to the right, a long hall with a living room and a bedroom side by side facing Dundas Street, and a kitchen opposite that led to the fire escape and the lane. He'd had a cot at the foot of his parents' bed beside the wall, near the door. One time his father had sat on the side of the cot and sung "Auld Lang Syne" and it had scared Rob, who knew he had been drinking and he would not stop when Lucy told him to and the next day his father had knelt before Rob in the kitchen and apologized: that kitchen with its yellowish walls where his father used to have "doubles" and "singles" — bread folded over, or kept in slices and dipped in the tea. It was in the kitchen his father had slapped him for having odd socks, and the fire escape was where his mother said his father had carried a fridge up on his own back — like Shiner.

But it was the hall he thought of now, looking down the long hall after coming in happily with his mother one Christmas, the freshness of the outside still on them, and seeing his father dialling for an ambulance. The ambulance that would take him away to die.

As he stood before the encrusted paraphernalia of sickness, Rob realized, for the first time, how his father had really looked: smaller when he had always seemed big, his broad shoulders in the pyjamas, the grey hair swept back on the sides, and his forehead, which had always stood out, even larger. What had surprised and alarmed Rob because it disrupted things — his father's fumbling at the phone, looking at them with what Rob thought was unnecessary alarm — Rob now saw as shock and desperation. He knew he was going to die.

His eyes, looking at them, so brown, dark, big. Rob had forgotten his eyes.

Lucy and Will used to sing and talk about eyes. Hers were blue, or hazel — "Beautiful, beautiful brown eyes." His father's mouth, thin Irish frog mouth, grim then.

That was December. The first time Will had gone to the hospital for tests, a sunny September, he drummed a freckled hand on the arm of a car seat as he waited with Rob in the new '54 Ford. His hand.

And sitting in school that fall looking at the clock in the morning, thinking his father was having an operation. The classroom. He was a little guy.

After Christmas dinner taking the turkey carcass into the blue dark bedroom to have him "examine" it with him: "Get it out, get it out, get it out, get it out!"

Was his cot in the room then? Where had he slept? Why couldn't he remember? After his father died the cot disappeared and he had shared his mother's bed. Certainly he remembered being in it and praying for Daddy to break a leg when Will went out one evening, standing outlined in the yellow doorway in a suit. Had Rob pouted, or cried?

The last day of January was when Will died. His mother by the phone, telling him, the bright, bright sun outside. Rob had the idea his father was taking a bath. Then he had cried and cried.

There were stories, how Will had asked the ambulance to stop outside the Christmas window at Eaton's on the way back to the hospital so he could see the Christmas lights and displays. How his last words were, "You're the best thing that ever happened to me," directed either at him or Lucy, it could vary. How Will's favourite song was "Danny Boy," and for a long time after Rob would weep whenever he heard it.

Only after he'd been told did he remember that he had put a little toy knight in his father's coffin. Had his mother suggested it? On his own he remembered thinking he saw his father move in the casket at the funeral parlour.

On the wall in front of him was a saint the size of a toy soldier, beside something from a medicinal bath — there was too much about baths. Vividly Rob remembered he had not liked it when his mother went out and his father gave him a bath, not as a little boy, not walking down the long hall to the blue-black bedroom while his father swung a belt behind him because he had done something wrong. "Wash between your legs." Was a witch going to come and get him?

Was it walking along, being looked at, lying face down across the bed?

Boom. The bass notes inside were bad.

◪

"You see, there is going to be an excavation."

Robbie listened to the talking. The priest had such a ripe, shiny face, peeled almost. His voice was musical, but insistent.

"Will that necessarily be a good thing?" Pearce did not back down from him.

Turning away so he would not quite make out the answer, Rob looked down the central aisle of the church. Though it was a humid, watery day, and not bright inside, he pictured himself lying on a bed by a plate glass window in late afternoon, scalding light coming in. By re-creating the nervous feeling he had when he "didn't feel like working out," was "lazy," or "didn't feel like going," he went to a familiar uneasiness. He never got that common, fluttery stomach before the actual fights; then he was eager. The bored anxiety he now created, yawning, stretching as he looked down the nave, diverted him. Abruptly he went out to join the men.

"Ah, here's the boy," said the priest, and then turned back to Pearce and went on in his lilting, familiar, intimidating way. "Now why wouldn't an archaeological excavation be a fine thing?"

"I'm not saying that," Pearce said. "But you're going to tear up that site."

"A cow patch."

"Well, it's special," said Pearce.

"We'll have a visitors centre, my friend. More people will come to the shrine."

"Will they?" said Pearce.

"Oh, they'll walk up the hill, some even doing the stations of the cross as they go." The assurance had a full tone, ever so slightly cynical, while remaining cheerful. "And we'll have a new retreat centre as well. Separate and private. You can leave your young pugilist with me to prepare himself for the coming trials."

"No," said Pearce.

"Want him all for yourself, do you?"

For the first time since he had know Stu, with his indoor skin, narrow skull and grey hair, Robbie saw him turn red. Not pink, red.

"What do you mean?" Stu said.

"An athlete must sacrifice," said the priest. "Isn't the boxer's preparation the hardest of all?"

"We have to go." Pearce paused. "Father." The joviality that had matched the priest's — Rob thought Pearce had actually been enjoying himself — might as well never have been.

"The dying Gaul," the priest said.

"What!"

"That's what you don't want, eh, bucko. Get him ready. Focus the mind."

"What sacrifice did you have in mind?" Pearce moved his left leg ahead, weight on his back foot, nearly in a boxing stance. He slid imperceptibly forward.

"None whatsoever." The priest coughed. "Unless you want to talk theology." And he spun away, his skirt swirling out, walking along a flagstone path to an adjacent building. The door he disappeared into remained open, showing a hallway of such polish the walls and floor gleamed. There was a crucifix on a wall.

"Unappetizing, eh?" said Pearce. "That's probably the refectory."

"The what?" Rob asked.

"The kitchen."

CHAPTER *14*

THEY HAD COME HOME from the cottage early and gone to Shiner's apartment and stayed there. Because he did not go out on Sunday night, the next morning, when Shiner announced, "Never had a hangover," Lucy worried. It meant he did have one.

"I can poach you some eggs," she said.

"Maybe that's my problem, I don't feel like eating." He went over to the kitchen sink to stand beside her and get the bottle of rye; Lucy delved into a steaming stainless steel pot. "But it's new, you understand." He patted himself with a balled hand just below the solar plexus. "I've got this hollow, like an itch."

"You just fall asleep when you drink." She was wearing one of his terrycloth robes and seemed very small in it.

"Like a hole." Shiner moved his hand as if he had indigestion.

"You eat well, and that's what's important. Do you want some eggs?"

"I don' give a shit." Shiner said it good-naturedly

enough, while managing to ignore her and concentrate on tipping rye into a glass. He filled his drink with tap water, which he did not let run; the liquid was cloudy.

"I'll get you some eggs."

Shiner took his drink into the living room and sprawled on the sofa, putting one pyjama-covered leg up on the arm rest. The red silk of his dressing gown spread around him. The television was already on.

"You'll let them just sit there," Lucy talked in the other room. "I'm not saying you won't eat them, but they'll sit there until eleven o'clock. Don't you have an appointment?"

"Lucy, an egg is an egg all morning."

"I'm glad you do eat them." She carried a plate in and set it down on the coffee table in front of him. He put his glass down beside the food, peering at the yellow of the butter on the toast, which was the faded colour of his drink. The yolks were brighter.

"Well," she said.

Drawing his chin in, which emphasized the squareness of his head and made him look stern, Shiner sat back up.

"You act like breakfast is already cold," she said.

He watched the TV.

"I know if I put them in front of you you'll eat them." She sat in a La-Z-Boy armchair that was at an angle to where Shiner had spread himself out. Both pieces of furniture faced the same way. Lucy tucked her legs up under her.

"I don't like this getting up in the middle of the night," he said.

"Oh." She cocked her head and leaned towards him.

"The old man used to do that. I could hear him in the middle of the night." Shiner concentrated on the television set.

"Oh." Elaborately, a little too casually, Lucy settled her heels under her body so she was half kneeling on them. "Is it drinking, or can't you sleep?"

"I've never slept all night."

"You can sleep anywhere, anytime," she said. "That's a gift, like Churchill."

"What?" Shiner frowned.

"The ability to nap," she said. "It allowed him —"

"The old bas'ard always got up early for work and he always managed to make just enough noise to wake everyone."

"But he didn't have to get up. He owned his own business."

"He drove rigs himself, eh."

"Was this in Niagara Falls, or Collingwood, or Haliburton?"

"What the hell difference does it make?"

"You haven't told me about that." She spoke wistfully, not looking at him any more, preoccupied and intrigued by this notion to explore. She said, "You haven't talked about that a lot. Tell me about it."

"What the hell for?"

Fussing with the rolled hem of her robe, Lucy uncovered her feet. "You know, Rocco's an attractive man."

"That dwarf."

"I mean he's a nice man, to Rob."

"He knows what side his bread is buttered on."

"I think it's more than that," she said and paused. "But I'm not sure about it."

"You know more than I do." Shifting his body as if he was about to stand up, Shiner spread both arms expansively over the back of the couch. "About the fight game he's connected, and he's cagey, and he's smart."

"Like you," she said.

"Christ, yes. You know, my old man got up in the middle of the night just like I do."

"You could have been one of those fur traders," she said.

"What the hell are you talking about now?"

"I was just thinking how you look in your tam, you're Scottish. Sitting around drinking with those other men on a porch. I can see you sitting around drinking, telling stories the way you and O'Driscoll do."

"My tam," Shiner said, then smiled. "O'Driscoll. That s-o-b. I don't curl."

"Insulting each other, really." Lucy pulled a ball of lint off the thick cloth where it was tight across her thighs. "Remember when I argued with O'Driscoll about whether you were handsome?"

"Jesus H. Christ."

"Tell me about your father," she said.

"Ninety-nine," Shiner answered one of the questions on the television quiz show.

"I know he started the business." Lucy reached around to push her toes more firmly under her, then looked down to where her nightdress puffed up out of her bosom. She brushed at it. "But he was a bit of an old meanie, wasn't he?"

"What do you mean?"

"I mean he was hard on you. It was you who really made the business go once you were in it."

"I drove the old White down to War-shington and I had to put a onion on my head, cut'n half, to keep my goddam eyes open."

"Why do you say Washington like that?" she said sharply. "It's like an old man."

"My father must have said it that way."

"It's so old."

Shiner shrugged.

"Did he hit you and your brothers?" She went a little dreamy.

"When I was twenty-goddam-five?"

"Or your mother?"

"Never."

"I got the impression from her he was an old meanie."

"Well, I mean, when we were goddam kids." Shiner paused and gave her his practised wolfish grin but with something different in it. "You saying we liked getting slapped around a bit?" His mouth curved, trying to involve her in a secret.

"No." She shook her head so hard her hair flew out.

"Eh?" Shiner tilted his head, questioning, insisting.

"That's not true." Her breathing was shallow.

"We liked it?" he probed, asking a question to which he was convinced he had the answer, satisfying himself.

"No." She got genuinely angry, and Shiner's attention went quickly back to the TV.

They sat quietly, and Lucy moved her gaze from his face out along his widespread arms to his fingers, blunt and clean, and the freckles on the backs of his hands.

"Shine."

He looked up.

"Rocco seems a gentle man."

"That leg breaker," he said. "Look, when I was a kid we had three squares a day and a roof over our head."

"I better take a bath," she said.

◥

When Robbie arrived at the apartment later that morning they were still in their bathrobes.

"Do you want some breakfast?" Lucy asked, lying back in her chair.

"No." Robbie gave the perplexed, disgusted look he often used when he thought he was hearing a stupid question.

"Did Mr. Rocco mind you staying all the way until Monday morning?" she asked.

"No."

"None of those characters has any job," Shiner said. "They could stay up there all week."

"Pearce is retired," Robbie said. "Jimmy works at the gym. Mr. Rocco has businesses."

"Some kinda business," Shiner said. "Bad business. Wop business."

Vaguely, Lucy thought of objecting, but she focused instead on Robbie's monosyllabic responses to her, registering them as adolescent, obnoxious. With her foot she nudged her plate towards him. "You can have my breakfast."

"It's eleven o'clock!" Rob said.

"You can have mine," Shiner said.

"Oh no you don't," Lucy said. "You're eating. You keep those eggs right there."

"What's up?" Rob said. "Why'd you phone for me to come over here?"

"Tell him." Using the arms of the chair to push herself forward, Lucy paused, then absented herself by walking into the kitchen. The skirts of her robe trailed behind her. But she kept involved; while turning on the tap into an empty sink she called out over its noise. "Are those bruises under your eyes? Are you tired?"

"I been fishing!" Robbie used the same affronted tone as before. "And Pearce and I went for a trip over to Martyrs' Shrine."

"I went there with Will," Lucy said.

Shiner said, "You been fishin'. You been ridin'. How come you look like a raccoon, then? Your mother's right. You look like you been takin' shots."

"That's from last week. I gotta go," Rob said.

"Maybe you shouldn't spar so much," Shiner said.

"You mean leave it all in the gym. I'm great for the nationals."

"You have to be brought along right."

"Pearce knows when we should start to taper," Robbie said.

"No, no. It's like a lottery, eh. Boxing, making the N.H.L., whatever. But if you hit the jackpot the payoff is enormous."

Robbie placed a fingertip under one eye. "This is nothing."

"Well, what happened to you?" Lucy returned, drying her hands on a tea towel.

"It's old," Rob said. "It's from —"

But Shiner woke up from momentary pondering and cut in. "Did I ever tell you about O'Driscoll's friend?" He looked at both of them. "He was a stock-broker."

"Like Will," Lucy said.

"A licensed stockbroker, not a customer's man," Shiner said. "Anyway, let me tell my story. This broker wants lessons, eh. Practically takes over the whole club to learn him boxing. A couple of hours a day for six months, just for him. I mean, you *knew* he was there when he was in the place. Then he arranged to have all his friends come to see an exhibition bout with him in it."

"Eat some breakfast," Lucy said.

"Pearce was there," Shiner said to Rob. "Okay. So the guy trains for six months, the show's arranged — he's got the whole office there."

Lucy asked, "Was that Marchment and Dunn, Shine?"

"Will you let me tell my story!"

"Eat something, then."

"Okay, the bell goes, and the sparring partner, the hired servant, comes out and throws a jab —"

"Those guys aren't servants," Rob said. "I mean, they'll carry you, sure, but —"

"Listen," Shiner said. "The broker didn't have time to be carried, because after the first jab —" Shiner came alive, his broad face creased — "because after the first jab he says 'Ouch!' — and calls the whole thing off!"

"Was . . . ?" Lucy didn't finish.

"'Ouch!'" Shiner nearly barked as he said it. "The guy told Pearce that he didn't know boxing was about getting hit!"

"Well," Robbie said seriously, "Pearce says that you won't last long if you do."

"Ah, Christ." Shiner waved a hand in disgust at the incomprehension in front of him.

Rob said, "I mean . . ."

"I mean," Shiner said, "I'm not talking about sitting in the front row with spit flying and —"

"Oh, Shine," Lucy said.

Shiner turned on her. "Well, that's happened to me."

"That's pros," Robbie said.

"That can be money," Shiner said.

"Not for opponents," Robbie said. "You don't want to wind up an opponent."

"Opponents," Shine said. "Who told you opponents? Rocco? What's he mean?"

"Opponents," Robbie said. "Guys whose career is professional opponents. Somebody you have to go through, get by. They pad your record. Pearce —"

"Didn't think it was about getting hit." Shiner shook his head. Then he crinkled his eyes up merrily and gave his own advice, going around whatever Pearce might have said. "You know what's good for kids, in something like boxing? You learn a shot in the head isn't the end of the world."

"If a guy looks bad," Rob said, "all marked up, you don't have to be scared of him. It means he's been hit; he's isn't hard to hit. Pearce —"

"Forget Pearce," Shiner said. "I'm talking general. It's good to know you can take a shot and it isn't the end of the world. Sure, it's unpleasant." He laughed at the memory of his story again, then said seriously, "It isn't the end of the world. You can take it and keep going."

"That didn't hurt." Rob jerked his head as if shaking off a punch. He smiled.

"I don't want you getting hurt," Lucy said.

"I guess I should get over to the gym," Robbie said.

"Since when do you work out this time of the morning?" Shiner asked.

"Are you going to train?" Lucy asked.

"Yes." Again Rob gave his forehead-wrinkling taken-aback look.

"I mean right now," Lucy said. "Don't be bold."

"Do you have to go now, right now?" Shiner said.

"I should get going," Rob said, but he didn't move. This seemed to be the longest talk he had ever had with Shiner.

"I bought Epsom salts for your bath," Lucy said to her son.

"I should get going," Robbie said.

"I'll tell him, then," Lucy spoke to Shiner, and turned to Robbie as if she was a doctor about to convey, patiently, simply, some grave news. "Uncle Shine is going to let us have the apartment."

"This one?" Robbie was animated.

"This one," Lucy confirmed, pleased with the effect.

"Shit!"

"Stop swearing," Lucy said. "You think you're like a big man when you swear like that. You can't swear. It doesn't look right on you."

"Dad swore," Robbie said.

"He didn't use that word. You're not your father. You're not a big man yet."

"Dad swore, Pearce swears, Shiner swears, Mr. Rocco swears, Jimmy —"

"Ain't human," Shiner said.

"He's only a boy." Lucy apologized generally. "It doesn't look right on him."

"That little girl." Shiner looked directly at Robbie; his right eye closed in a squint. "When she says . . . If she wants . . . You better not . . . That little girl . . ."

"Where will you live?" Robbie asked Shiner.

"Milton," Lucy answered for him. "There's an apartment over the garage in Milton."

"Over the garage." Robbie frowned.

"What, you're worried about my space?" Shiner said.

"It's big," Lucy said, "much bigger than here."

"But your business," Robbie said.

"You think I'm going broke on you? I'll be *at* the business now," Shiner said. "Canadian Truck Lease."

"I meant —"

"Lease instead of Transport," Lucy spoke up. "And you won't have to sleep on the couch like I make you do when I'm over here." Lucy made it clear she was conveying common knowledge of where Shiner always slept in his own apartment when she visited. The fiction was for Robbie, but he managed to almost believe what she said and skip over it.

"Great." Robbie said it neutrally, thinking what the change in living arrangements would mean. Then he lit up. "Two-bedroom 901." He looked around. "My own room. Thanks, Uncle Shine. I mean it."

CHAPTER *15*

AS ROB STRETCHED on the carpet of the hotel room, Pearce supporting his arms behind his head, Lucy walked towards him pointing her finger. Rob tried to look past to the open door and the corridor.

With his usual reflex, Pearce asked himself why she was here, not bothering to answer. He couldn't even fake resignation, though he tried. Shoving off Rob's shoulders, which had tightened, he got up and peered around for Shiner. "Mrs. Blackstone," he said.

"Where's Shine?" Rob dropped his arms, took slow breaths.

Arm still out, finger extended, Lucy tottered towards them, heels sinking in the rug.

At her approach, Rob tilted his face upward, smiling a strained, friendly greeting. "Your finger's crooked," he said between his teeth.

Lucy looked at the tip of her hand. Astonished, she turned huge, questioning eyes at them both, but her mute question — "Why has time transfigured me?" — was solely for Rob. "I hadn't noticed," she said.

Fleetingly, so fleetingly, the boy's tight, hard, Vaseline-shiny faced collapsed. "What do you want me to do about it?" The words were almost gargled in his throat as he spoke.

"Marvellous," Pearce said when he saw the effect on Rob. "It can't be arthritis, Mrs. Blackstone."

Expectantly, she looked to them again, and drawing the offending arm back clutched it into her bosom. "What happened?"

There was no answer. The fur stole dropped off a shoulder, leaving it bare. In the act of pulling the garment back up tight around her, Lucy disregarded the shadows that had just passed over her face. Smiling her usual extreme social smile, tucking her chin in modestly, she fussed with her wrap. "Hello, Stu," she said.

"The Canadian Championships," said Pearce. "Here we are."

"I'm all set," Rob said.

"The youngest lightweight ever to win," Pearce said.

"I should be with the boys," Robbie said to his mother. In the bathroom Jimmy was filling a bucket with ice. Two other lads from the club, about Rob's age, were sitting on the bed; a policeman who sometimes coached with Pearce was laying tape out on the top of a dressing table.

"But you are," Lucy said.

Pearce expected her to say "darling," then he realized she never used such endearments, not with Robbie, or Shiner. Maybe he'd heard her say "honey." "It's kind of hectic," he explained to her.

Suddenly Rob's face twisted with frustration; there was a furrow between his eyes, his lips parted, he looked like he was going to cry. But before Pearce could say anything he went flat again. "Where's Shine?"

"Getting a venue like this was his idea," she said. "The sponsorship. And the association bought it."

"It's a good idea," Pearce said.

"I should go." She was reacting to Rob — as sensitive as he was to her, she responded equally. "I wanted to wish you well, honey."

Yes, Pearce thought, she uses "honey."

"Don't call me that," Rob said, but in a comfortable, automatic way. "Where *is* Shine?"

"Out front with Mr. Rocco. They both want to be proud of you."

"And they will be, they will be, Mrs. Blackstone," Pearce said.

"We're in the front row," she said.

"You look nice, Mum," Rob said.

"We're all set." Pearce slapped his pant leg. He said to Lucy, "Strategy, eh, you have to know what to do. We're all in his corner."

"The big dance," Rob said.

"A dance," she said. "It isn't a dance."

"Just another fight," Pearce said.

"The big dance." Her indignation was mild.

"You know," Rob prodded good-naturedly.

"You'll have to do more than dance," Lucy said.

"All night long!" Jimmy walked into the suite with his full bucket of ice. "We gonna dance?"

"All night long," Rob leaped up and started to shadow box.

"Can he win if he's dancing away?" Lucy asked.

"He can do anything." Jimmy looked at her vibrantly.

"Plant and dance," Pearce said. "He'll throw, don't worry."

"Stay busy, eh, Stu?" Rob said.

"Here, son, I should wrap your hands."

"I have to warm up," Robbie said to his mother.

"We're ready," Pearce assured her.

◢

At the end of the first round there was a solid leather thump, like a clash of heads with helmets on. It sounded like a collision — but Pearce had his head turned away, ever so briefly, at the time. The audience he had glanced back at was in near darkness. "That's the hardest he's been hit," he said to Jimmy.

"What?" Jimmy ignored him, his face turned to the ring in a kind of frowning rapture; the white fluorescent lights highlighted the broken bridge of his nose, his brownish-blond stubble.

The beginning of the round had been surprisingly quiet for an amateur championship, the boys feeling each other out like pros. Then the lad from Halifax rushed in, leaning forward too far, off balance, but throwing extremely hard left hands.

Rob had not stepped forward, blocked the hook with a right forearm; he did not chop back a right. He seemed puzzled, not knowing what to do; he got on the ropes and leaned too far back.

"Get outa there," Pearce barked.

But Rob leaned even farther back, consternation showing on his face. His opponent stepped sideways, tried to break loose as Rob brought his arms forward and tried to grab him. An uppercut smashed through Robbie's gloves, then another. They didn't connect completely, but Robbie looked like he was trying to clutch the rising spear pole of his opponent's forearm. His eyes flew up, the whites showing. Then, luckily, he got his left glove in the other fighter's right armpit, and his opponent couldn't swing. The referee broke the clinch, warning the kid from Halifax to keep his head up. "Watch the butts," Pearce added, and the ref waved a finger as a warning about coaching from the corner.

The ropes of the ring were very loose. "They unscrewed the goddam turnbuckle," Pearce said to Jimmy. "Somebody unscrewed the turnbuckle. I didn't check."

Jimmy flicked a hand at Pearce. "Forget it. He'll be okay if he turns it up a notch."

"Even if the other guy isn't landing, coming forward like that is aggression." Pearce said. "They're supposed to count scoring blows, but they'll count aggression. I know it. I know it. The other guy's carrying the fight. Rob hasn't done anything."

"He threw a good left hand," Jimmy said, but didn't go on. The hook Rob had thrown had whistled, been extremely strong, but it had missed. It was painfully obvious that Rob had never met an opponent this muscularly charged and determined. The circling, the feinting he had done, or tried to do, was legitimate. If Rob fired and missed, he could get hit extremely hard.

"I'm going to figure this out," Pearce said.

"Rob don't want to punch himself out," Jimmy said.

"You idiot!" Pearce said. "This isn't ten rounds! He's got six minutes to get going."

Pearce was afraid. Robbie had reason to be afraid. "I'm sorry," Pearce said to Jimmy.

"I boxed, you didn't," Jimmy said.

"Yes, I —"

"Let's get him goddam going," Jimmy interrupted. "Either he's in a fight or he isn't. He's got to step up."

The bell went and Rob came in. His face was blotched. Jimmy handled the stool, stood to his side and gave him water. Pearce knelt in front.

"How you feeling?"

"Okay."

"You've got to get busy, son," Pearce said. "Hit him coming in. He's messy but you don't need to hang on and let him hit at you. Keep out of the corner, but if you get caught, blast out. But hit him coming in."

"He's hard to hit." Rob was breathing more deeply than he should have been. Jimmy tipped the taped neck of the water bottle to his lips, but only brushed them with drops of liquid. He wiped snot from under his nose.

"Can you get busy?" Pearce said.

"Yeah."

"No problem," Pearce said. "Just give me this round. Three minutes. A straight right as he's coming in. It's that simple."

"Okay," Rob said.

"Pile driver," Jimmy said.

The bell went.

The charged movement of the first round was gone, but the other fighter kept coming, and instead of combinations Rob would throw one hard punch to stop him. But both men hit forearms, biceps; they jumbled together and clung, the other always seeming the stronger.

"He's not putting anything together," Jimmy said.

"He's afraid. He's holding on," Pearce said.

"I don't know what he's waiting for," Jimmy said, "Come on, Rob!" he called. Now the referee warned Jimmy.

"Right hand," Pearce said, loud enough to be heard but glancing sideways to avoid eye contact should the ref look their way, as if the instruction came from behind him.

"He has to throw more than a right hand," Jimmy said. "Even if he can't put them together he's got to fire. That isn't even defence."

"I zee someting."

"What!" Jimmy said.

"Louis–Schmeling. Schmeling saw how Louis dropped his left hand as he threw his right. That's how he hammered him."

"That's it, perfesser, you tell 'em."

"I will."

"And what did Louis do to him in the second fight?" Jimmy asked, all the time watching the ring.

"It's easy to say, isn't it?" Pearce admitted. "But we're not up in there with that eggbeater."

"The guy is awkward," Jimmy admitted.

"It's like he's just charging," Pearce said. "And wanting to get Rob with his elbows as he follows through."

"He's following through," Jimmy said.

Then Rob did connect with a right as his opponent came in. The other boxer leaned back, pawing with his gloves; he regained his balance, adjusted his helmet, and surged forward again. Rob had not pressed his brief advantage, just standing in front of the other guy, as if giving him a moment.

"This is a fight without jabs," Pearce said.

Again the bell.

Jimmy was silent and grim as they got into the ring.

Pearce knelt in front of Robbie. "Now you have to do something," he said to him.

"The guy's crazy," Rob said.

"That's all right," Pearce said. "But you have to win. And to win you have to let your hands go. Don't worry, just get busy. If you get busy you can win. Do you understand me? Don't think about anything but this round, last round. But you have to throw punches."

"The steam's out of him," Jimmy said. "He's slapping now. He was slapping when you got him good there."

"He's not slapping," Robbie said.

"Look at me," Pearce said.

Robbie did so as Jimmy gave him more water. This time the boy took a mouthful and only took his eyes off Pearce to spit it out.

"Let your hands go! Left, slip, right hand, left. Okay. Throw."

Now Rob smiled at someone at ringside. The smile was forced. In the background Lucy and Shiner and Rocco were standing, both men in double-breasted topcoats, Shiner's the usual beige. Lucy was looking around, showing evident displeasure at the way things were going, her fur shiny in the dark crowd.

"Look at me," Pearce said.

The boy was.

"C'mon, Rob. Listen. Let your hands go, son, let them go."

"Let's find out about his chin," Jimmy said.

Pearce focused on Rob's eyes. "You have to throw punches."

It wasn't so much that the other fighter was punched out, he came on as before, but the sense of an inexhaustible explosion had gone. Rob still went back to the ropes, covered up, but he punched out of the crouch as he had not done before, stooping forward, his behind nearly sitting on the middle rope. The other fighter stumbled as he backed off; before coming in again he high-stepped, pranced as a ghost of exhaustion touched him. Rob drove a left hand between his opponent's throat and chin, twisting his head. They came together, but this time didn't lock, and the other man seemed to let both hands down at once, awkwardly, as if he was going to look around to see what was going on. Rob hit him with another clubbing left, and then with what Pearce would later call a projectile the size of a fist in a glove, a short, straight right on the chin.

The other fighter's mouthpiece came half out, giving him a stupid smile, and Rob lashed a long left hand to the side of his face.

Waving his hands, the referee stepped in.

"It's over," Pearce said.

But it wasn't. Rob was waved to a neutral corner. The standing count began.

"It *has* to be over," Pearce said to Jimmy. "I don't know about those first two rounds."

Then it was over. The referee looked at the other lad's face, the O of his open mouth as he nodded that he wanted to continue, and waved a finish. There was a step towards Rob to show a desire to keep going, but no protest when the referee guided the boy from Halifax towards his corner.

"He was done," Jimmy said. "It's the right thing. He lost it fast, though."

"Rob won," Pearce said.

◪

That did not seem enough for Lucy. She pursed her mouth and ignored Shiner and Rocco as they jumped around. From the illuminated ring Rob looked down to his mother and wondered if she was disappointed because he had not effortlessly dominated the whole fight. She kept her mouth contracted in a puckered, tight way. Her head looked about to quiver slightly, the look of someone overtaxed, fed up, who didn't find anything funny in the situation, who demanded cajoling, but who would not be moved.

Rob smiled. Lucy cast a glance around to see who was watching, then took some formal credit with a half nod and her public smile, though it was more tense than usual. Immediately Rob got out of the ring and went over to her, flanked by Jimmy and Pearce. At his approach she looked away again, upset. Lucy swallowed: preoccupation, self-pity, frustration were tightening her throat. Rob would have to take responsibility for it.

"You fought a tough kid," Rocco said. "You did all right."

Shiner was exuberant. "Hey, well done. Now don't complain, Doctor." He beamed at Pearce.

"I'm not complaining." Pearce watched Lucy: she's expecting an excuse which she won't accept, he thought. We won't give her one. The boy isn't superhuman. "A good outcome and good experience. Come on, son." He put his hand to the small of Robbie's back to steer him towards his dressing room.

"Bad night," Robbie said to his mother. "I couldn't get going."

"Hey, you took him out," Jimmy said.

Lucy disapproved very publicly; she made it clear she had come to a point where she did not want to hear any more.

"It turned out right in the end," Pearce said, thinking of how this boy had performed in other fights. If there had been excuses before, at any time, they had been good ones. And there had hardly been any.

"I couldn't get going," Rob said.

"Hell," Shiner said. "You stopped him."

"He was a step up," Rocco said. "You did okay." He greeted someone in the crowd.

The men could ignore Lucy, but Robbie was as agitated as she was. He was about to persist with his mother, querulous now, when, completely unexpected, as if he wanted to stop whatever was going on, Jimmy reached over and grabbed Lucy's face in both hands.

He gave her a smacking kiss.

"Merry Christmas!" he said — the holiday was half a year away. "Congratulations!"

CHAPTER *16*

"HIS MOUTH WAS OPEN when he kissed me, yuck." A tremor shook Lucy's body and she balled her fists, crossing them up under her throat.

Emerging from the tiny bedroom he now had in Shiner's old apartment, Robbie looked at his mother. His hair was mussed, his face swollen.

"What?" he said, though he had heard every word, and he knew she was talking about Jimmy. "I don't want to know about it. I don't want to know about it."

It was as if she'd been waiting for him, but she didn't say anything more and turned to go down the hall.

In the bathroom, shucking the robe he'd worn at the fight last night, he examined a purplish bruise on his right shoulder, then looked at it again in the mirror. He tried to stay all soft and sore, to let himself be hollow, empty. He couldn't. Seeing a shaving mug of Shiner's on the sink, he felt like knocking it over. He didn't, and looked closely at his face, suddenly tensing it completely, and making a guttural noise of fury and impotence at what he'd heard.

It didn't stop the feelings. He couldn't be alone by floating away; anger made it worse. He picked up his discarded covering and put it back on, didn't bother to wash, and stalked out to confront his mother.

"Why'd you let him do it?"

"Me let him!"

"Why?" All the cords in his neck were showing.

"It was like that horrible man at Shiner's Christmas party," she said.

"Christmas, why is everybody talkin' about goddam Christmas?" Rob said. "Jimmy's talking Christmas, you're talking Christmas. It's summertime, or springtime. I don't know."

"Don't swear," she said precisely, though lisping rather than biting at the words. "That client of his was repulsive. I hate that kind of thing."

"I don't want to know about it!"

"It was Christmas. People kiss at Christmas, people get kissed at Christmas, he was kissing me goodbye. How was I to know he'd open his mouth like that?" Then she added, "He hugged me too close."

"I don't want to know about it. Then why'd you let him?"

"I didn't *let* him. It was a party. I had to say goodbye."

"But why'd you let him? Where was Shine?"

"Right beside me."

Robbie grunted the words out. "Why do I have to do something about this?"

"You don't. You're talking like a child."

"You let him in front of everyone," Rob said.

"Of course it was in front of everyone. It was in front of everyone last night. You were there."

"I don't want to know. Not every lady gets kissed like that."

"Every lady! I'm your mother. What was I supposed to do?"

"I meant at Shiner's. Jimmy just, he just . . . he wanted to stop stuff."

"What stuff? Your friend Jimmy —"

"You know I can't be friends with him now," Rob said.

"He's hopeless. He's hopeless anyway. So is that Pearce."

"No, he's not!" Robbie said.

"You stop it! Just stop it." Lucy never seemed to shout at Rob, but this time she was close to it. She nearly spit the last three words, ending whatever they were talking about.

Suddenly, in contrast to what he had always done — fighting back or walking away or ignoring her — Robbie's eyes filled with tears and he said, "I'm sorry. I'm so sorry, Mum."

This grief took Lucy aback. "But you haven't done anything wrong."

"I'm sorry about everything." Robbie surprised himself. "I'm sorry."

"You didn't do anything, honey."

"I know I let you down." He sobbed dramatically, as if to work himself up the way he had when he was little.

Lucy knew how crying increased crying. "It's okay, honey."

The reassurance seemed to be what they both wanted.

Her calm put him at a distance, and his tears stopped. "I don't know," he said.

"It's okay. You go get cleaned up."

"Thanks," he said.

When he had gone she called after him, "We'll go to the party."

At the club there were balloons, one in each corner of the ring, and processed cheese on platters, which Pearce was carrying around.

"Strange time for a reception," Shiner said to Rocco as they stood together, not having removed their topcoats. "Afternoon. And nothing to drink."

"Yeah, well," Rocco said. He looked different from the night before; a colour like putty showed beneath skin that was usually so plum dark. His aftershave, which Shiner could smell, seemed too sweet.

"Nothing to drink." Shiner took a step back. "Well, what can you expect from the old maid that organized it?"

Pearce, dressed in white shirt and black flannels, just like he was a referee except there was no bow tie, came up to offer a tray.

"Where's the bar?" Shiner asked as he approached.

"Oh, no bar," Pearce sang out, smiling in a glittering way. "You know that," he emphasized melodically. He was half aware that his subtle, silvery aggression made him sound a little like that predatory priest at the Martyrs' Shrine, but he didn't care.

"Balloons," Shiner snorted. "The place is like a kids' birthday party."

"Should we call him 'The Kid,' Mr. Rocco?" Pearce smiled all the harder, and turned his pointed charm away from Shiner. "He's certainly young enough."

"Sure," Rocco said.

"You hung-over?" Shiner asked Rocco.

"You don't ask people that." With a frown of distaste, Rocco turned his back on Shiner.

"Why not?" Shiner ignored Rocco's gruffness and looked around.

Pearce noticed the smaller man's broad back was stooped. "Are you all right, sir?" he asked.

"A little indigestion." Rocco said it with a faint voice.

Over came Jimmy, looking as if he had been up all night. "Some show, yesterday, eh?" he said.

"Well." Rocco shrugged. "He knows how to win."

"You can say that again." Jimmy squinted one eye shut and peered with the other. He hadn't shaved and, because of his brushcut, nearly his whole head seemed grizzled.

"Hey, Jimmers," Shine said, friendly enough but too familiar, obviously about to bear down about the night before. "Jumpy Jimmy, what was the idea of —?"

"Cheese?" Pearce pushed the big plate between Jimmy and the other two men.

"I had one hundred and seventy-one amateur fights, eh," Jimmy said.

"That so," Rocco said. "You couldn't have won 'em all."

Wiping his hand across his face, using his hand like a washcloth, Jimmy said, "That's only amateur, eh. I was what you call a gutsy fighter. And I could knock you out." He peered at Shiner.

The tray dropped with a clang. "Oh, dear," Pearce said. "I'm just not mechanical." He was talking in the singsong he'd affected since the beginning of the party. There was less defensiveness and more of a warning, concern even, in his voice now.

"You're clumsy," Shiner said.

Pearce let the comment go, and continued, "Put anything in my hands, put a clock in my hands, and it seems to fall apart. I think I'll come back in the next life a plumber." Then he paused and asserted flatly, "I seem to be all right with cuts, though."

"Is that so," Shiner said. "At least when you talk about cuts you talk normal, instead of like some kind of goddam Mick headwaiter."

Rocco cleared his throat. "You have something against Catholics?" he asked Shiner.

"I got nothing against 'em. What's with you?"

Pearce bent to pick up the cheese.

"I don't know what I ate," Rocco said, tapping his chest.

"You're lucky you didn't eat this slop." Shiner nudged a wedge of cheese with his toe.

"I could knock you out," Jimmy said to Shiner again.

"You could knock me out, eh?" Shiner said. "But I bet you can't keep quiet for a minute. One minute."

"I could knock you out."

"One minute." Shiner made an elaborate reach to uncover his wrist and look at his watch. "I'll time you." His watch and cufflinks were both gold.

"The champ!" Jimmy exclaimed, seeing Robbie and his mother across the room. He forgot about Shiner and went over to them.

"One hundred and seventy-one amateur fights, and how many as a pro?" Rocco asked. "Messed up." He stated it, rather than asked it of Pearce, who had risen.

"How many fights did you have, sir?" Pearce asked.

"What's with the 'sir'?" Shiner asked. "There you go again."

"Forty-five," Rocco answered.

"And it didn't do anything to you?" Pearce said.

"The guy's crazy," Shiner said. "He's simple. Look at him."

Slowly, flat-footed, his left foot inching forward, his right food dragging up to it, Jimmy advanced on Robbie and his mother. His head was cocked merrily, his fists low at his waist. "Champ," he said.

◪

Seldom did Shiner comment on Lucy's appearance, even when she asked him, but this time, when she finally did come over, he loudly noticed her smile. "Why's your lip drawn up so high that it's touching your nose?"

During the progress she made towards them the men had noticed Lucy's smile, perhaps a little more straightened than usual. When she heard what he said she stopped.

"You look like a rabbit." Shiner tugged at his French cuffs and waited for general approval, but he didn't get it. Jimmy was back at his side again.

"That little girl," Shiner said, as if it was an explanation, then again, "That little girl."

"I'll knock you out," Jimmy said. "I'll break your nose." The words cascaded.

"You're outa line, pal," Shiner said.

"But he's good with kids." Pearce stepped between Jimmy and Shiner, speaking to Rocco. "Even if he does want them to start sparring at eight."

Expelling air through his nose, Rocco gruffly agreed. Then he relented and said gently, "I think we all started at eight."

"Try and hit me," Jimmy said to Shiner.

"I don't want to hit you. You some kind of idiot? 'Hit me.'"

"Hit me." Jimmy kept his head still, a steady target. "Try and hit me."

"I don't want to hit you," Shiner said again. "I want you to shut up for a minute, for thirty seconds."

"I'm an idiot," Jimmy said, nearly closing one red eye with a thin, overhanging fold of flesh, and raising his chin.

Shiner looked down at the misshapen face, the bridge of his nose sunken, one eye a slit, the other too wide. He didn't say anything.

"Come on, lead at me."

"Oh, get lost," Shiner said.

"All right, then, you bastard," Jimmy said.

"No!" Lucy flung herself forward. Her black pumps kicked out behind her and she fell into Rocco, who held her.

Small cherub mouth set in a wet O, Jimmy gave his left hand a slight flick, like he was brushing at a fly, and then brought his right over with deadly serious-ness towards Shiner's temple.

"Jim." Pearce hadn't meant to grab Jimmy, only tap him, but because of the shift of Jimmy's body as the punch was being delivered, Pearce's hand opened and pressed down on Jimmy's shoulder. Shiner was tall. So Jimmy missed slightly and landed full on the side of Shiner's face.

"I'll cool you!" Jimmy yelled.

Off balance and shocked, Shiner looked around. "Rob!" he called.

"Not the boy," Pearce said.

Stutter-stepping sideways, Shiner pushed Pearce into Jimmy; it was the kind of bullying push one child uses against another to challenge him to a school-yard fight.

And then Robbie was there. In complete contrast to the way Jimmy had gone after Shiner, the small man and Robbie started to throw their hands at each other in a kind of slapping contest.

"Girl fight!" Shiner said.

Carefully Rocco tried to set Lucy aside, though she clung to him. "No," Rocco said to Shiner. "They don't want to hurt each other. And the kid's defending you."

Because Lucy and Rocco were the same height, dressed alike in formal blue with white shirts, and nearly entangled, Shiner had the impression of them as a couple.

"Let the little bitch go," he said.

"Shine," she said as he towered above everyone and held his jaw.

With a strong pull towards Jimmy and Robbie as he freed himself, Rocco spun on Shiner. His limbs were free, and as stiffly as if it had been set in a cast he bent his short left arm. Up went Rocco's right reflexively to guard his own face. Transferring his weight, he lunged up and clipped Shiner on the tip of his jaw.

They both went down, Rocco holding on to his left shoulder as pain shot down his arm. Rob turned from Jimmy, though he was still reared back as if avoiding blows, looked at his mother and then Rocco.

The older man sat down in a nest of navy broad-cloth, his heavy head hanging.

CHAPTER _17_

SOME OF THE RIBBONS at the back of his hospital gown had loosened, so that when Rocco sat up the smock gathered in front of him like an enormous bib. Pearce could sense rather than see his hairy, humped back. But Rocco smiled, and didn't seem sorry for himself in any way. I'll feel that for both of us, Pearce thought, I'm older than he is.

"You could tell with fighters they weren't trying to hurt each other," Pearce said of Jimmy and Robbie. "The way they went at it."

Rocco shrugged. He'd said the same thing.

"I read once that Joe Louis and Sugar Ray Robinson — I think it was at a USO show or something — had at each other like that. Some words, then a flurry sort of, I'm not sure how it was described, a mix-up, a mess — no one hurt."

"You read," Rocco said with contempt. "You never saw it."

"Yes," Pearce insisted, "I read. And what puzzled me when I read it was two knowledgeable athletes like that, going at each other, and no one hurt. It was like nothing. And now I've seen it."

"Two pros," Rocco said.

"Jimmy was a pro," Pearce said. "It's the principle, if you see what I mean, the idea I'm trying to get at. Like I said, maybe they didn't want to hurt each other."

"Maybe somebody broke them up," Rocco said, meaning Robinson and Louis.

"Yes."

"Fights can be a bad thing."

"Oh, yes."

"The thing to do, however, once they start, is to win them."

"But did Jimmy or Robbie want to win?" Pearce said.

Rocco smacked one fist into another with such sharp authority that for the first time Pearce could see the truth of what he had heard and never quite believed about Rocco: he was a brawler. Especially when boozing. Pearce had never seen him take a drink, but sensed in him something that could be intransigent, heedless, ruthless. He pictured him drunk at the Rex, wordless vowels in a loose mouth, feigning retreat while shaking off a restraining hand — then driving somebody.

"And how is *Mr.* Maclean?" Rocco asked.

"Fine. And how are you?" Pearce said it with transparent concern.

"The thing is" — Rocco avoided looking at Pearce — "when you have short arms you have to get inside." Then he added, "My hand is the size of a grapefruit. And I guess my heart isn't so good."

"Bare hands can be a bad thing," Pearce said. "Open hands."

"That isn't what you just said about your boys."

"I was talking about intention there," Pearce said.

"Yeah," Rocco said. "Well, what was the kid's *intention* going after Jimmy no matter how out of line he was? The nut was only trying to defend his mother."

"But his mother's involved with Shiner," Pearce said. "His mother didn't want Shiner hurt. So he does what his mother wants. Don't think they're not close, in spite of the boy's wriggling to grow up. Robbie's everything in the world to Lucy. Don't think she doesn't let him know it."

"Shiner could win, you know," Rocco said.

"I just hope we don't have to get rid of Jimmy," Pearce said.

"Ah, these things happen," Rocco said, dismissing the ruckus that had landed him here.

"How about getting rid of Shine?" Pearce said.

"C'mon." Rocco nearly whispered; the effect was that of a soft counterpunch, showing that Rocco understood quite well, if at a level beyond words, the ties that bound Robbie and Lucy and Shine. "But he could be taught a lesson, about how to treat people. Schooltime," Rocco hissed.

◢

Pearce was still at Rocco's bedside when Lucy visited. The men had been talking about how high the hospital bill would be, another reason for Rocco to get discharged as fast as he could. Wearily, Pearce added, "But you don't want to rush things."

"Shine's hired me on" were her first words. As

usual, as always, she was "dressed," as Pearce put it, with makeup and mascara, though her blonde hair was so clean and fluffed that it appeared thin in the diluted atmosphere of pale walls, fluorescence, and daylight that filled the sick room.

"I gotta go," Pearce said, rising.

Though Lucy was a small woman, her presence made Rocco seem even smaller in bed, still powerful though, a gnome forming himself into the shape of a bowling ball.

"We were just talking about cost," Rocco said.

"You look nice," Pearce said to her, meaning it and feeling sorry for her at the same time.

"You old horse trader, you," she said to Rocco, "you'll be out on the street in an hour."

This was said with such obvious bravery that both men wondered if Lucy was on the verge of tears.

"It's —"

"He could be out this afternoon," Pearce said.

"It won't take you long," Lucy said, holding something back while managing to ignore Rocco, the condition he was in.

Now he knows he's really going to die, Pearce thought.

"I was thinking about Robbie," Rocco said to her, as if it had been on his mind all day. "You know, sure he needs polish, and can't be rushed too quickly, but he actually could make a lot of money."

"Hey, slow down," Pearce said. "Anyway, we'll talk later. I should get to the gym. I have to clean up."

"That's like saying you gotta rush home to sweep the floor," Rocco said. "Stick around."

Smiling at Lucy, Pearce sank back into his vinyl

chair, which exhaled with his weight. She remained standing at the foot of the bed.

"We should get things settled after last night," Rocco said.

"When Will died I thought I would never get out of debt, ever," she said. "He'd just bought a new car."

"A flat-head Ford," Pearce said. "Rob told me."

"Ever," she said. "Until Shine came along. Before him there were . . . I was at my wits' end. If Will hadn't gotten into a veterans' hospital before he . . . He knew Donald Fleming, a cabinet minister, Donald Fleming knew him and got him into Sunnybrook."

"It is tough," Pearce said.

"He didn't have a pension," Lucy said. "Insurance. Not at a brokerage house."

"No." Pearce added a bitterness he felt was not only his to what she said. "Not on Bay Street."

"He was just a customer's man," she said.

"There ain't any security," Rocco said.

"You haven't done badly," Pearce said. "Better than my safe job."

"This is costing me an arm and a leg!" Rocco said.

"Nothing." Lucy started a list. "I didn't know what I'd do with Rob. I had no job."

"Didn't you have a small business?" Pearce said. "Not so good, I know, but . . ."

"Selling bridal china and crystal!" Lucy said. "I didn't know what I was going to do. It's the truth."

She didn't seem at all like she was going to cry now, and yet both Pearce and Rocco moved closer to her, Pearce standing up again, Rocco shuffling forward on his hams, keeping the sheet on his lap, feeling very high up on the raised bed.

When you were at ringside and looked up the fighters seemed all legs.

He could remember only the light — that wasn't true either — but the light overhead and faces at ringside peering through sheets of rain-grey darkness, and all about the noise and beyond darker still.

Not just the light, but being under it, and bright blue in the other guy's eyes that wasn't alive, and you knew you had him. Or those brown buttons looking at him steady, too steady, and his manager saying, "What corner you want my guy to go to when he knocks yours down?" and getting a reaction. Solly always said some little thing.

When you were up there it was you that was tall; he was thinking this way because Rocco realized he'd been watching now for thirty years. That time in the '40s going into the Palais Pier and at the far end of a dim aisle, really not that far back but it had seemed it, there had been two heavyweights and, like something Pearce once said, they were like infants, except long, reaching for, hitting at each other, not quite in slow motion.

Then you got close, and it wasn't slow motion, and those guys were both really so tall and pale with red streaks on slick wet skin.

The water that spilled in the corner; flat leather soles slipping on it, getting an uppercut in when Savat slipped and went down. All the talk then!

Robbie was like him, he'd tear out the ring post if he needed to hit you. Maybe he wasn't.

The Newsboys League, Police Station Number

Two, long gone, his brother taking him to it, and loving it, even at the very start: "Paperweights, one round."

And being anxious for it. And being in it once it started: being in it — watching his arms, his eyes, watching out, getting in, slipping, getting out of there. Hurting him. Wanting to win. Getting hit one time so he saw three guys at once in front of him. If that was the worst it wasn't so bad — except for that kidney punch from Willie Simms that paralyzed him all down one side. Ahhhhh. And they'd been sparring.

"Stick 'em" Willie Simms. "Why'd you do that, Will?" Rocco had gone right after him. Rocco sparred with middleweights.

Willie hadn't been afraid either, none of us had, why was that? Telling Rocco all that personal stuff, about his family: "So I said to her, Marva, get fixed! We'd lost two kids already. Ain't nothing wrong with me!"

"Nice to meet ya, Willie."

The story about his wife getting her tubes tied was practically the first words Willie said to him. He'd tell you anything.

Briefly, Willie had worked for him, after he'd wrestled that year and boxing was finished. When offering him the work, Rocco had been told, "My brother's a bad guy, eh."

Quickly Rocco wondered if he was being insulted. "What do you mean?" he'd asked.

"He has prostitutes, in Chinatown." But Rocco saw Willie was simply talking, like he always did. "That's no good, beating up women to get what you want. I had a girl said she'd do it for me, said she knew how to do it" — Rocco recalled the falsetto voice Willie used to imitate a woman — "but I said no way, I'll make my own money."

And Willie had, getting up and running ten miles every morning, then slugging eighty-pound doors all day, then working for ten bucks a round as a sparring partner.

Rocco knew Willie could collect, because he'd been told he'd done it for his brother — "He's a bad guy but he's my brother, but I don't like him" — but he wasn't really any good. "All I do is pin their arm behind their back and it's over," Willie told him. Yes, it was over, but the money wasn't always there.

Why the hell did he call himself "Stick 'em"? Willie could hit with power.

Then Willie had his stroke, but instead of road-work he walked every morning for an hour, and he still saw him around and he was still alive. "How ya doin', Willie."

"My boy's in plumbers college."

Willie was alive, and Rocco knew how the bad brother had died. "At forty-eight, I saw him drinkin' wine with bugs in it!" One side of Willie's face odd, but talking away. "The women left him! A woman will only put up with only so much after a while. Bugs." Then Willie nudged Rocco to look up at the girl carrying around the ring card. "She hefty."

Aside from Robbie's bouts that was the last fight he'd been to.

You couldn't say Willie went too far. That's how he was. And Rocco kept thinking, alive.

Had Rocco really been able not to be hurt? He put his hand on his hairy stomach, which still felt hard under what he jiggled. Of course he'd been hurt, Willie had hurt him. But he hurt them back.

Again he said to himself, Robbie was like that, and again, maybe he wasn't.

Something would have to be done about Shiner.

CHAPTER *18*

AT THE MILTON PLACE THERE WERE at least six broken motorcycles, along with a car hood, an engine block, and rusted lawnmowers lying out in the yard that surrounded the cinderblock building. The gravel was so sparse it was more like dried mud with stones, Lucy thought. Some of the two-wheeled machines were gutted. Behind them was a field too green in the June sun, looking chemical, overfertilized; far beyond it a line of pale trees, then the highway. Small cars going by the escarpment.

Lucy drew heavy drapes, pastel with big purple flowers on them. She turned to face the silence of the air-conditioned room. Even the idle trucks outside looked dirty, she thought, though Shiner always said, "Keep 'em on the road, don't keep 'em clean." But the rigs weren't on the road, and there weren't any employees around.

Shiner was always clean; he changed his underwear every day. This apartment was almost like a showroom. But there was so much: at least six stereos and none of them working, five china cabinets without china, no chesterfields except a right-angled sofa in one corner. There were two big TV sets and a tall home entertainment centre; four or five coffee tables; the banana-yellow one had volumes from an encyclopaedia of crime, ordered by Shiner from a late-night TV show, spread across its surface.

The layout at the Milton, Ontario, headquarters was this one huge room over the garage, its front door leading out to an office that ran the width of the building, while the back was divided into a bedroom and kitchen. The kitchen was spotless, she'd wiped around it herself first thing on arriving, and empty, except for dented cans of Lima beans, which must have come from a broken shipment.

When she arrived at noon Lucy sensed that Shiner was still sleeping, even though he usually got up every morning. She didn't want to wake him, but finally went over to tap on the pale mock maple of his closed door.

"Honey," she called. No matter how softly she knocked her knuckle seemed to hurt.

"Yeah," came from inside. "Okay," muffled.

Retreating across the room, noticing how thick this carpet was compared to the last place, Lucy awaited him by the drapes. From where she stood she could smell, mildly, the Pine Sol she'd used.

It took a while, she wondered if he was having a shower, but then Shiner came out of the bedroom scratching his head. He had not bathed.

"How was the drive?" he asked.

The leather maroon slippers, which she had given him, were scuffed, she saw, down at the heel. That was not like Shiner; his clothes always seemed new on him. With his colour it didn't show if he didn't shave, but she knew he hadn't. Her heart fluttered; the slippers, she realized, were exactly like the ones Will had on the time he'd called for an ambulance. Those were also a gift from her. Will's had fewer scars.

"You look like you've seen a ghost," he said. "What's up?"

The V that showed of his bare chest was pale, a little grey. Was he getting grey hair there? Wilson's usual orange-pink skin looked different, there was the slightest sheen on it — from being in bed too long?

In spite of the space and polish and the size of the objects around her, everything suddenly seemed a mess.

"Where's the Maclean coat of arms?" Lucy asked. She'd given him that as well. In the old place it had one wall, the biggest wall, all to itself.

"I dunno, what's the matter?" Walking towards her.

"I've been to see Rocco." Lucy noticed the tautness beneath the soft material of his dressing gown as he got close, then he was pressing against her, and she could feel him. Easily, Shiner took one of her arms and put it behind her back, in a loose hammerlock. It made her arch against him. His other hand reached down to lift her skirt. Her breathing quickened.

"You think I give a shit," he whispered into her collar and hair and perfume. "He's dead."

Opening his mouth wide, wider than he ever had before, Shiner ran his tongue all over; it was as if he was holding half her neck in his mouth.

"Don't." She twisted away a little. "Mr. Rocco —"

"Is dead." His voice was muffled. Then Shiner

pushed her away. "Mr. Rocco." Shiner mocked the name. As soon as she'd said "don't" he'd stopped. Now he stepped back as if he'd been doing her a favour. Her throat was wet.

"Wait, Shine," she said, and caught him; he stood, docile enough, as she examined him. "Let me see your face."

In the cleft of his jaw — she ran her palm up and down his bristles — in that dimple she loved, there was some crusted blood. "Let me, hold on." Lucy touched the scab.

"From Mr. Rocco?" she asked as she went to her purse and retrieved a hankie. It was strongly impregnated with her scent, and Shiner turned his head slightly as she brought it up to his face. Then she spit on it and he jerked sideways as she tried to put the wet point to the cut. Firmly, Lucy brought his head back around. "Don't you like Mum's spit?" She smiled indulgently. "You're just like Robbie, squirming at Mum's spit, he calls it." As Lucy concentrated on what she was doing, she chewed her lips.

"Robbie —" he took her wrist and held it firmly away "— has to do better. This thing is getting all screwed up."

"He's only fifteen, for godsake." Lucy looked from his chin to his eyes. "Rocco says he could make a lot of money."

"Sooner, rather than later," Shiner said. "That's the handle, don't you see? How old he is. Anyways, we have to straighten things out. Jimmy —"

"Is gone, will be gone," Lucy finished for him.

"Yep. And how sick is Rocco? We have to get moving."

"Where's Ben?" Lucy referred to Shiner's office manager. "Where is everybody?"

"It's only this week," Shiner explained his quiet business. Then, "Rio Algom's no goddam good."

"Where are the ore samples? Downstairs? They're too dusty for the house."

"Ore samples! What the hell does that have to do with anything? Ore samples. They're no goddam good. You mean those samples I showed you?" Shiner recalled rolling them out of a potato bag onto a wet floor. "Who the hell knows where they are? They're junk."

"It will be all right, won't it?" She sounded like a mother asking a specialist about a sick child. There was in her question a will so profound that any other answer than the one she wanted would mean that there could be no God.

"Yes, it'll be all right." Shiner let her wrist drop and scratched his head again. "You want to put some tea on?" And he added, "It's just a temporary suspension around here. I've got the contract from Dominion Steel, but it doesn't start till the end of the month, and I don't want to extend the line of credit."

He had never told her this much before. Her lips parted, and Lucy put her hand behind Shiner's neck. Relaxing, he leaned back into it.

"All I'm saying is, it won't hurt if Robbie gets crackin'," Shiner said. "The angle is that he's just won, the angle is his age."

They came together. She made a very small, reluctant noise.

"It's like you like to say no." Shiner felt her breathe deeply against him, felt her rib cage expand and her waist shrink. As they kissed her mouth opened and her tongue was so soft against his.

She pulled away. "I'm not seventeen, you know." Then she said, "Don't," and kissed him again. His robe fell open; he was naked underneath. Lucy put her face into his chest as he began to undo her front buttons. "You smell like vegetable soup," she said.

◤

"He really thinks Robbie has a future." Looking exactly as she had when she arrived, in her suit with the A-line skirt and narrow lapels, Lucy sipped tea on one section of the sofa. Arms spread wide in that way he had, big freckled fingers around a drink, legs splayed, Shiner faced her. He was still not dressed. His bare feet were on the rug; his bare shins were shiny.

"He does," Shiner said.

As the cup left her lips, Lucy made a face; there was no milk. "I should go shopping," she said. They seemed isolated from time and daylight. If she went outside it would be late, the sun would hurt her eyes. "You need some things."

"What's that wop ever done about his future?" Shiner asked. "Who needs him?"

"For the connections," Lucy answered. "You said so yourself."

"Connections," Shiner scoffed. "That old woman Pearce has done everything."

"Up to now," Lucy said. The rye and water in Shiner's fist, that he cradled with such familiarity, suddenly alarmed her. Usually the way Shiner handled a glass was reassuring, but the colour in this one, deep yellow, nearly brown, repelled her. Surely there was more than half rye there, much more.

"We'll have to keep a closer eye on that guy too," Shiner said. "Until he's history."

"Who?"

"Pearce. Jeeze, what am I talking about?"

"Don't you like anyone?" she said.

"It isn't about like, it's about trust. *Mr.* Rocco." The disdain was exactly as before. "You sound like the kid."

"I taught him to say sir and ma'am. I require that."

"You require that."

"Absolutely."

"*Mr.* Rocco."

Lucy controlled her impatience. She knew it would be best if he dropped it on his own. She controlled her breathing, then sighed a little when he said, almost reluctantly, "I've never heard Rob say ma'am, and he sure as hell doesn't call me sir."

That was something they could talk about! With an instant delight that surprised her, she thought about buying Shiner a tie for Father's Day and saying that Rob got it for him. No, she'd get something special, something a boy would think of: an ornamental mace, a ball and chain.

"For heaven's sakes," she said, "you're too close to him to be called sir. He respects you. He calls you Uncle Shine."

"He think that up on his own? How many other uncles has he had?"

Now she was hurt, and showed it. "You're close to him."

Shiner didn't answer. He seemed stunned. Maybe he really was drunk.

"I know Rob and I are special . . . ," but she stopped when Shiner continued to sit there numb. She wanted a response, any response, and said, "I think Robbie trusts Rocco. They went fishing."

"Fishing!" Shiner woke up. "Are we even talking together here? That happened what, twice or something? He have us all up to that shack twice or something?"

"It's hardly a shack. And it seemed to mean a lot to Robbie. Why didn't you take him then?"

"I've never even been alone with him."

"Why didn't you take him when we went to Ben's place?"

"I was with you!"

Lucy didn't say anything.

"Anyway, it was really me brought Rocco in," Shiner said.

"And now you want him out." She was angry.

"Slow down. Say, you know I told the kid not to play the trumpet."

"He wasn't serious about that anyway," Lucy said.

"Now he doesn't have to fight to protect his mouth all the time. But I tell you, if he keeps up like that performance the other night he'll look like he's got a permanent mouthpiece."

"His lip wasn't swollen." She was close to tears. Pulling her legs up under her onto the couch so she was kneeling on her heels, Lucy put her face into her hands and hankie. But her mind changed. "He won, didn't he," nearly snarling from her position of prayer and glaring at Shiner.

"Hey," Shiner said, though he still didn't make a move towards her, not to comfort her, not to calm her down. Finally, still immobile, he gritted his teeth and said, "Damn."

Then he got up and went to her.

CHAPTER *19*

"THIS PLACE IS LIKE A MORGUE." Wayne McCarroll slipped at the lip of one of the mechanics' pits. The empty garage of Canadian Truck Lease seemed as cavernous as an airplane hangar. Hot, dusty light flooded through the open doors; the parking lot outside looked baked.

"Grease monkey trap, by the Christ," said Jerry "Butterball" Cook. In spite of his good humour, irritation crept into his voice. "Don't fall." Oil had sunk into the very cement of the steps leading down to the long, concrete, coffin-shaped ditch. "A shop teacher I had did, by Christ, and is he all crippled up, for life, son, all twisty necked and gimpy. Messed up."

Both men wore shiny suits and slippery shoes, and the obvious, ringing fact that there was no one else around aroused their instincts and lent a celebratory quality to all they did and said. Both were from an out-of-town local, both had been drinking. They were there to deliver a message to Shiner, but were in no hurry to find him.

"Should we look for the way upstairs?" Cook said.

He grinned foolishly, but did want to get on with the job. A Newfoundlander, childhood memories of work not quite complete and hence unpaid for made him the more serious, if not the less exuberant, of the two.

"Christ!" McCarroll slipped again, laughing, close to doing a pratfall, but his arms swung so violently in exaggeration that Cook suddenly grew annoyed. He thought what he saw was stupid, but a dim warning bell about a real lack of control in McCarroll's behaviour went off. They could mess up themselves.

"Cut it out," Cook said. "Let's find the turkey."

"His car's outside, the Merc, right?" McCarroll said, then, trying to stop his laughter from subsiding, said, "Ya Newfie prick, ya."

"The other one has to be the broad's," Cook said.

"Then let's go find 'em."

◢

They didn't need a key.

The living room, close to the size of the garage downstairs, and with its sense of cool, still, sealed quiet, made them hesitate.

In a far corner they observed a curve of bare flesh, red cloth gathered and bunched around its base; all they could see was this hump of round-shouldered back, and to each side part of a woman's legs and stockinged feet. The deep blue of the nylons was in striking contrast to the flame of material and bowed, creamy skin above them.

This tableau was eerily silent, with barely any perceptible movement, yet it had a desperate quality to it.

Later both men would wonder why they hadn't

stopped to watch; they didn't, but strode right over, and yelled as they went.

"Suck boy!" called Jerry Cook.

The bulk above Lucy shifted.

Wayne McCarroll followed with "Galboy! Punk," although the tall, nude, semi-flabby man who turned to greet them was quite the opposite of a galboy — those vulnerable adolescents turned into "wives" and "bitches" and "ho's" by means of prison gang rape. A shadow of the word "boss" crossed their minds. Though the guy was bug eyed, grim lines ran down from the corners of his mouth.

It also occurred to both men later that it shouldn't have started the way it did, though they never asked themselves what difference it would have made had they not launched into action.

Fumbling at his waist, Shiner seemed to be searching for the cord to close his robe. Very quickly he realized it had dropped off and that he wore no clothes.

Cook launched himself forward, fists flying in an almost circular, beating motion. This was his style, this was how he fought, how he had fought since he was a youngster and had been called fat: swarming in with fists and weight. His successes had been great.

Lucy had curled into the foetal position on the couch while McCarroll stood on the periphery, half kicking, just flicking, his straight-last shoes in their direction as Cook tore into Shiner. He glanced back and forth between the grappling men and Lucy's behind, which seemed aimed at him.

Did she say something — it would have been "Shine" — muffled into the pillows?

Never would McCarroll have thought he was embarrassed, and he gave a grin, then a laugh; but his laugh was loud and witless.

The resistance Cook met surprised him. An impression of a slightly soft body with a brick-red face above it was mistaken altogether. Briefly Shiner had raised his chin contentiously, like an inexperienced fighter, and Cook landed rapidly; Shiner's hands slipped on his head as he tried to grab Cook's hair. Then, all the while getting hit, Shiner got a thumb near Cook's eye, and Cook felt the force and intention of the gouge. He had to turn his head away. Shiner seized his arm at the biceps, stopping the blows from that side, and gathered strength for a shove. Then Shiner punched, and landed a lucky one that brought his knuckles hard against Cook's collarbone. Jerry raised both hands to protect his throat. Reeling, naked, swinging wildly and off balance, in panic and desperation, Shiner threw punch after punch. "Get into the bedroom!" he yelled at Lucy. "Get the tire iron."

McCarroll didn't think about stopping her, she was moving slowly anyway; he was still grinning stupidly, not realizing what was happening to Jerry. "Throw him down and kick him in the head." He barked out the old formula, as if talking to himself, then, "You wanna shoot the boots, asshole?"

Legs braced wide, Shiner stumbled barefoot.

Elegantly lifting his knee and firing, McCarroll landed a hard square toe to the back of the ribs.

Shiner's whole body was red now. McCarroll's blow left no mark.

Cook reeled backward. McCarroll got Shiner in the spine.

In spite of confused, urgent glancing around, and in spite of pulling her skirt down by the hem, almost as if she was tidying up, Lucy got into the bedroom quickly enough. Purposefully, alertly, she searched, all the while thinking: Will used to say that, "tire iron"; "Get the tire iron," shouting it in the car when he knew he kept it himself under the front seat. He'd never drawn it out, never used it. Remembering this made her sense that Shiner slept with it beside his bed. There it was.

"Break his arm" was something else Will had said, about these kinds of people. And "lock all the doors in the car at night, at stoplights." Will had talked about this kind of thing. It never happened. Were they trying to break Shiner's arm? In contemplating this, almost meditatively, she did not consider that they had not actually got hold of him.

He'd lied to her, Shiner had lied to her. They weren't downstairs; there, in a heavy canvas bag, were the ore samples. Grabbing them — they looked too heavy to lift though they were not — she dragged them with one arm, the tire iron in the other, out to the living room.

"You know the trouble with you, you got no respect," Cook was spluttering and spitting, backed off from Shiner; the strength he'd encountered, wiry — which should have been in a smaller frame — but utterly unbending, and big, big boned, had shocked him completely. As did Shiner's reaction now: ignoring Cook and his words, he ran awkwardly, clomping, wild eyed and naked towards Lucy, hands outstretched for what she held.

McCarroll took a step forward as if to trip his opponent; he wasn't close to him.

Wordlessly, so intent that he embarrassed his attackers — like some pervert fumbling at a kid's fly or something, not to be denied, nuts — Shiner took the sack from Lucy and swung it wildly it over his head. The tire iron was in his other hand.

"Help!" Shiner advanced on the intruders.

"Crazy bitch," Cook meant Shiner, and though he did have a suspicion Shiner was acting, and feinted another lunge, he wound up back-pedalling.

"Keep your goddam mouth shut, bitch," McCarroll said as they retreated.

"Help!" at the top of his voice. One end of the bag flew open, and small alarm clocks, like projectiles, flew all over the room.

One hit furniture with a plastic clump; carpet and fabric absorbed the shock of the others.

Suits shimmering, faces jerking imprecations at Shiner, Cook and McCarroll seemed to slither out the door and out of the room.

"I thought you'd lied to me," Lucy said. "I thought you had the ore samples in your bedroom all along."

"Shit, no." Shiner lifted the collapsed khaki and looked at it dumbly. "Why?"

Linking him as if they were strolling, Lucy walked Shiner arm in arm back to where they had been, leaning against him.

CHAPTER *20*

THE NEWS HAD COME, and it had come from Shiner, that Jimmy was to be eased out. "What else can he expect," Shiner had asked Pearce, "carrying on like that? The lady's uncomfortable. That guy really does need a rubber room. You're the brains, anyway."

Pearce wished he could let the whole thing drop — for he was going to tell Jimmy — just like he wished he could drop the ridiculous implement that hung from his right hand. He'd been examining the thing, taking it apart, when the doorbell rang.

There was Jimmy, looking as if he'd been dancing around as he waited. "What time is it?" Jimmy said with great animation.

"Why, fight time," Pearce said.

"What time is it?" Fist driving through empty air.

"Fight time! Come on in."

"What, you gonna shoot me, Stu?"

A cord was coiled around Pearce's forearm like a wrist guard. The appliance was shaped like a drill;

black, with a bright red suction cup attached to a metal extension that would have held the bit.

"Can you believe this?" His finger on the trigger, Pearce waved the thing around.

"What is it?"

"Rob's. Rob brought it in. It's a massager. Said it's his mother's."

"A massager." Jimmy's brushcut had grown out, and he'd slicked his hair back this morning, so it stood straight up and spiky. This effort, even if he was unshaven, made Pearce's heart sink.

"An electric massager. With attachments."

"It's a massager, all right," Jimmy said. "His mother's massager. You bring it home to give it a try yourself."

Jimmy's scorn was like a gift: the quick, suppressed, angry reaction Pearce felt allowed him to stay with why he had asked Jimmy over. "Get in here," he said, though that felt too tender. "Come on in."

They went through the dim corridor of Pearce's front hall and emerged in a big empty kitchen, filled with the morning. Jimmy shaded his eyes.

"Look at that," he said, then, "There it is," gesturing to the table where the box lay open. Some attachments were still in their slots, which contoured their shape; others were scattered around. One, an octagon, stood on legs of many little flexible protuberances; there was a round knob, and a pointed knob. A mushroom head lay on its side and quivered with their footsteps. All were red.

"You're taking it apart," Jimmy said.

"No, I'm not," Pearce said.

"You're lookin' at everything."

"Sure I am," Pearce said. "Sit down."

As he took his place at the table Jimmy cleared off the loose pieces with his forearm.

"Do you want some tea?" Pearce knelt to pick them up.

"Got any coffee?"

"Instant okay?"

"Yeah."

"I'm not sure she even knows he took it." Pearce went to boil water. "I'll tell him to take it back."

"Givin' that to a kid," Jimmy said.

"He doesn't know what it's for. Maybe she doesn't or she wouldn't have shown it to him."

"It's a vibrator," Jimmy said. "Lookit the picture."

On the cover of the box was a blissful young woman in a ponytail, the machine pointed at her neck.

"A rabbit punch is a damaging thing," Pearce said. "Maybe this would work well on those muscles."

"You believe the broad uses this on her neck? Who give it to her, Shiner?"

"Yes," Pearce said. "She told Rob."

"Don't tell me you aren't planning to have a go on it yourself."

This was the furthest Jimmy had ever gone. Compassion drained out of Pearce. At the same time he felt as alone as he ever had in his life.

"You think I'm like Shiner." Pearce made no attempt to keep the disappointment out of his voice. "About Robbie."

Jimmy squeezed what was left of the bridge of his nose with thumb and forefinger.

"You're mad at the world," Pearce said. "The boy doesn't know halfway to heaven about this gadget, maybe we don't either."

"Please," said Jimmy.

"This isn't about me, partner," Pearce said. "Don't be mad at me. We can only do what we can do. And I don't think she intentionally gave this to Robbie, if she gave it to him at all."

"So it's her problem, eh," Jimmy said. "To hell with it all and the kid, she's got a problem, so to hell with it all."

"No."

"Well, her problems get to be his problems, in case you haven't noticed."

"Why'd you get into boxin', pal?"

"Whaddaya mean?"

"I mean, there's a lot wrong with it, a lot, if you see what I mean. But it's a great thing, or it can be a great thing, can't it?"

"Sure." Jimmy withdrew, but his face seemed to swell; his lips worked back and forth over each other and Pearce wondered if he might weep.

"There's courage, however misplaced. And there are rules. Why, when a guy's a goof in the ring, does it bother us so much? Because it isn't fair? Because there is no justice? But where else is there justice? You can only do the best that you can."

"I got into it for the money," Jimmy said.

"At the beginning? I don't think so."   .

"What's that got to do with things going to hell in a handbasket?"

"And embrace." Pearce was aware he looked as if he was gazing into the far distance, that to say these disconnected words made him look abstracted, ridiculous; but he said them.

"What?" Though irritated, Jimmy didn't half hear him.

"You've seen it after incredible fights. The guys hug each other."

"That's bullshit. A lot of that is such bullshit. I been there," Jimmy said.

"Okay. But there is something, isn't there? And whatever is there could get wrecked. That's why you're so upset."

"No!" Denying whatever Pearce was talking about, which seemed to have so little to do with how he had acted, and with what he was feeling, Jimmy deliberately, minutely, tightened the muscles of his neck and head. The trembling that resulted was an intense, repelled, rejection.

"Why's the fight crowd seem so much more, I don't know, interesting isn't the word . . . welcoming?" Pearce went on persuasively, though taking note of the cords, the different colours, the swollen vein by Jimmy's throat. Were they even friends any more? What was he doing? "Christ," he said, knowing he had lost wherever it was he was trying to go.

"They ain't," Jimmy said.

"Because they don't have to prove they're tough? I've heard it explained that way."

"'Cause they're poor." Jimmy said it like a question.

"You're a tough guy, Jimmy."

"What about takin' care of the talent?"

"For ourselves. Is that it?" Pearce asked.

Recklessly, Jimmy got up from the table.

"We have to do it the right way," Pearce insisted.

◢

Telling Jimmy he would not be needed had actually scared Pearce. After sitting back down the little man started talking in a kind of blurred monotone, around whatever he was trying to say, slurring. Whatever point Pearce was trying to make about boxing looked like a silly justification for brain damage now. If Jim had stayed in the game a few more years I'd be cutting up his meat for him, he thought. In daylight scar tissue showed shiny around Jimmy's brows; what had once been dimples were now lines in the flesh of his cheeks. His jaw hardly moved, but Pearce could watch its outline.

Since he wanted to keep coming around to the fights, Pearce had said okay, knowing he couldn't do anything about it anyway, just as he couldn't keep him out of the gym, nor would he want to. The worry was that Jimmy's presence at events would be one always on the edge of vision, would always have to be accounted for. Giving permission created the sense of an agreement entered into; they would not have to note, then ignore, his defiance, or think of him as lurking around afterwards. He could be acknowledged, "dropped by to say hello, eh," included but neutralized. Readily agreeing he should not work the corner after his troubles with Lucy and Shiner, Jimmy more reluctantly said he would pull back at the club. But he'd be around.

◢

"Get away!" clearly, angrily. Pearce could hear it in the corridor. "Don't you have anything else to do!"

"Ah," teasing, cajoling.

"Get away!" really angry now, but some sort of conclusion had been reached.

Pearce knocked. The door to 901 opened.

Behind Lucy, quickly, Pearce saw Rob slip out of the room. He'd expected to see Shiner.

"Oh." She paused. "Stu."

"I thought I'd drop this off," he said. "I don't think it's suitable."

Taking the massage kit from his hand without even seeming to notice, Lucy said, "Did you hear what happened to Shine and me?"

"Was I supposed to?" He was not asked across the threshold. "Rob didn't tell me anything."

"They came down hard on him." She whispered this, a phrase she was obviously repeating. Then she told Pearce a version of the attack in Milton, leaving out how they had been found and making it sound as if Shiner, by walking out bravely, tire iron at his side, had faced the intruders down. "We think it was Rocco sent those men," Lucy concluded.

Pearce winced, as if to say, "That's rough." "Are you sure?" he asked. Oh yes, he thought, though Shiner had other troubles. At the docks a bag of sugar had fallen, or been dropped, from an unloading ship and narrowly missed his head. The story had come from Shiner himself. A reddish double chin in an orthopaedic collar, Pearce thought; Shine with a crooked neck for the rest of his life.

Lucy didn't answer, but with one hand on the doorknob, blocking the entrance, she looked as if retelling what had happened made her want to bounce on the balls of her feet. Anticipation, but for what? Pearce thought. What can I say?

"That's terrible." He looked at her. "I'm sorry."

Eager and conspiratorial, Lucy waited. Pearce was ready to be indignant, ready to be angry at what he saw was her assumption, all along, that she would be protected. That's why she could make a story of what had happened, why she didn't seem to take it seriously enough: she assumed that she would be taken care of; it wouldn't touch her in any way. How Shiner must have resented that.

Pearce was wrong, and saw it at once. Wanting more from her, and sensing, almost lewdly, that whatever she said would allow him to see into her, to a shining creature revealed, bright lit for his examination, was illusion. Why, she was like Rob. Just because they didn't react — and the gossipy, wicked excitement of her story was a lack of reaction — didn't mean they didn't feel. He sensed how deeply she had been affected. Rob's silences, her breathless sharing, they were the same thing. And Lucy carried a weight of anxiety, blind, deaf though it seemed, that must have made aspects of her interior life unalterably bleak.

Pearce was not invited in.

◢

Sitting on his mother's quilted bedspread, Robbie was glad he could not hear Pearce's voice in the living room. He did not want to be included. He would see Pearce later at the gym.

That empty feeling of waiting for a workout, of not knowing what he would do until then, all day, overcame him.

His hand rested on a silk blouse she had thrown across the covers. Grey light came in through the bamboo curtains. Something like fine plaster dust, the colour of the daylight, lay on the wide window ledge. It always seemed to be there. Before him, on her dresser, were a silver-backed brush and thin bracelets, necklaces, tiny chains, and other things, trays of them. There was a silver-backed handmirror, and a black hat, her church hat, with a veil.

After his father had died Lucy joined the Catholic church. Monsignor Petipaw had been awfully good to her when Will was sick, and helped her, with money and other things. She told him that. He also knew about her lessons at St. Paul's. When he was sent to a Catholic school, Brother Richard and Brother Terrance, especially Brother Terrance, helped him. That was the first two years. Later came the ones who hit. But now he just thought about the hat, and how he had felt when she told him that women had to wear hats, had to keep their heads covered, when they were in church. Words couldn't explain it. He felt sorry for her? Why did they have to? Did little girls? He pictured a group of women, each one looking like Lucy, in black with short skirts, all of them putting their hands up to hold the hat on as if they were walking into a wind. Were their eyes down when they made that gesture, did they look up and sideways to see where they were going? There was no wind in church. Lucy wasn't a Catholic any more.

Emile Griffin was a hatmaker, in New York. Did he live with his mother? Maybe Pearce had told him he did. In an apartment overlooking the streets, an old shiny wood apartment with open windows but higher up than the one Robbie had been born in. How did Robbie know where he lived? He didn't; he knew he was imagining it, but he did know that Benny "Kid" Paret made fun of Emile Griffin for making hats and that Emile Griffin had beaten him to death for it. Hung him up on the ropes and the ref didn't stop it. Emile Griffin was very dark with a wide rubbery face and muscular. How did he know that? He didn't. Maybe he had seen it in *Ring* magazine. The feeling, the bass notes came. With hooded eyes, feeling so weak but with his soft mouth both grim and bitter, Robbie wondered where he was, if he was even there.

CHAPTER *21*

IT'S GOING TO GET WORSE. Pearce kept his mouth shut and tugged clumsily at Robbie's hands, trying to get his gloves off. It's as if I can't be trusted to do the job any more; she's here all the time.

"Untie 'em, Stu," Robbie said. "They're not undone."

"I know." Pearce fumbled at the laces, and while he did so Robbie turned away from him and spoke over his shoulder to his mother. "You don't need to do my laundry!" She was on the other side of the gym.

"Stand still." Pearce was faced by the white, recently widened, pillar of his neck. It was thicker — those wrestler's bridges seemed to work.

"But it's a fresh singlet." Lucy held the folded garment out like an offering.

"No," Robbie said.

She walked over.

"Let me get this!" Pearce created a knot. Since Jimmy was gone, both Lucy and Shiner had taken to showing up at the gym a lot more. But at least Shiner missed some of the training sessions.

Jerking loose, Robbie stalked away, though with a self-absorbed spring in his step, pushing up off his toes. He can't be that upset, Pearce thought. There was a light sweat on his shoulders, giving them a sheen. The cotton of his shirt was barely stained.

"Take responsibility." Pearce blocked and confronted Lucy when she reached him. He smiled. "Do it yourself, I tell them. You have to pack that bag!"

"Here," she said. "I washed it this morning."

On the floor by the medicine ball, by the situp board, Robbie waited, holding his knees. No one else was training.

If Jimmy was still around to help he'd divert this, or would he? Pearce wondered.

Lucy handed him the fresh shirt.

◪

Though less than the mother, which is how Pearce thought of her now, Shiner was still there an awful lot. With a new formality — he didn't even take his topcoat off when he sat down — Shiner and Lucy would occupy the alcove of moulded plastic chairs that now seemed to form the centre of the gym. Plump hands on well-tailored knees, leaning forward, or sitting straight up, large and unsmiling, Shiner watched. Though she could occasionally look fraught and distracted, Lucy had a newly acquired stillness when he was there. It seemed hard won. A shadow would pass, she would gnaw, compress, twist, or purse her lips, then sit, detached and apart from all that was going on. In her separateness she remained one of a couple.

The two always kept a vacant seat between them. With the wide skirts she had taken to wearing, Lucy seemed smaller than before, smaller than ever. No other parents or athletes ever occupied that space when they were there.

"It's like everybody else is undressed," Jimmy once muttered from the scales where he lurked at the back of the room.

"Well, we are," said the boxer whose weight he was taking.

If what had happened in Milton came from Rocco, and surely it must have, Pearce thought, the warning has only made Shiner more stubborn. Rocco was never around any more, but Pearce was convinced it was not out of fear.

"It's no way to run an operation," Pearce had taken to muttering.

"What's that?" Rob had asked him, more than once.

"Nothing," Pearce always said, thinking, The boy can't even take a breath unsupervised. The parental presence also meant that Pearce had more work; he felt obliged to go over and explain what he was doing, while Rob was left idle, without Jimmy.

Finally the boy asked: "Where is Mr. Rocco?" He'd been told about, and accepted, Jimmy's dismissal.

"He's sick, son." Pearce didn't look up from the duct tape he was winding around a torn glove one of the little guys could use after school. "You know he had a bit of a heart attack." It was no damn good; Pearce threw shapeless leather back into a communal box under the timers' table.

"Can I go see him?"

"I'm not sure the hospital will let you in." In spite of himself Pearce imagined Lucy and Shiner overhearing what he was saying. They were too far away, but he resented feeling he had to talk for their benefit.

"That's the way it was with my dad," Rob said. "I couldn't go see him, at St. Michael's." He seemed to accept it, but Pearce knew he wouldn't have, even as a little tyke: outside a first-floor window, looking in curiously from the street, or in the lobby, before a statue with an upraised sword, the small boy would have wanted to see his father.

"This isn't because you're too young. You have to be a relative, I think. Why do you want to go see him, anyway? I'm not sure but he's been discharged already."

"He's Mr. Rocco," Robbie said.

Having taken forever to inquire, and seeming to mutely accept Rocco's, not absence, for he had never been that much of a presence in his life, but apparent inconsequence, the boy now said his name with such dignity and respect that Pearce looked at his bare flesh, searching for goosebumps. There were none. He was the one feeling them.

It was hard to think of Rocco the man, who he really was, the way he'd disappeared. Was Rob used to this, had other men just gone out of his life? He thought of boyfriends of his mother's before Shiner. No, it was simply, as infrequent as their contact had been, that Rocco was important. A gesture, a kindness; it meant a lot to Rob.

"He's still thinking of you," Pearce said.

"How do you know?"

"I really think that's true." To a point, he thought, not like me, but true.

◥

"Amateur night is over" was the way the change was announced, by Shiner, and at the age of sixteen Robbie Blackstone had his first professional fight.

Four rounds.

Pearce went along quietly enough. He would often say "No good will come of it" to himself, telling the words over and over; what this incantation really suggested, however, was the opposite. Repeating his negative little prayer made him immune to it. Only one more round.

They prepared as usual, Pearce as always stressing the technical. He never, never had, talked of fear, of channelling fear or anything like that, and he did not want the jump Rob was about to take to feel momentous.

It wouldn't be. The opponent, an aging amateur champion — who had not stayed on the national team long, and never quite made the Olympics, nor progressed in the professional ranks — was well known to Pearce. He knew his tendency to pose, his weaknesses.

Rob carved him up. A small cut opened over the left eye of the older man in the first round, sure enough after one of his hesitations, and then Rob seemed to get the jab in every time, and Pearce meant every time, twisting his glove at the extension of his punch. His jab was so fast, and long, but Pearce had the impression he was grinding and twisting leather into the wound. The contest following Rob's was delayed because of the amount of restorative stitching the ringside doctor felt he had to do. No one had shown Robbie how to open a cut like that.

The next fight didn't tell much. Frankie McIlwain

cancelled, and a Romanian — Shiner called him a Bohemian — who was making his own professional debut was put in and if anyone didn't want to be where he found himself it was that frightened, slope-shouldered, beetle-browed sleepwalker. Out came Rob: bob bob, hands tight to the side of his head, bob bob, uppercut, and it was over. A towel was thrown in, there were boos, but the dread and paralysis of the man who'd been knocked down made him look incapable of making a fist, let alone holding his hands up. Didn't come to fight? Didn't show up? He was hardly present, Pearce thought, oh my. As unsatisfying to the audience as it might have been, ending it then was the only thing to do.

Quite a few people didn't see the punch, and afterward Rob had to explain it over and over: uppercut — swinging his arm as he said it — on the chin.

The crowd was quite a bit larger.

Danny McNair might have been considered too big a jump, but Pearce thought Rob could at least stay away from him if he had to, and agreed to the match. There was some guilt attached to Pearce's consent. He knew Rob would need a lot of help from his corner to beat Danny. Bigger than Rob — everyone he fought seemed bigger than Rob — McNair was a fighter with whom strategy was a necessity. But winning by decision, because that was what Rob would have to do, was what they needed. As a corrective, Pearce thought, a modifier. The trajectory of success the boy was enjoying was safe, but Danny would bring it down a little. It wasn't really a gamble: Robbie could keep out of trouble, he'd never stand toe to toe; but he'd have to listen.

Every time he fought Danny seemed to bring his extended family with him. He was from Buffalo, but seemed to have a lot of relatives in Toronto. Bug-eyed, exhorting those at ringside to cheers and chants, jabbering and dancing and cutting up, Danny always put on a show. Delicate stretch marks, faintly grey green on his round brown arms, glissading down his shoulders and back, showed how he continually made weight too quickly. "Suspect" was too generous a word for his training. But he could be dangerous. If his flesh shook as he shadow boxed and shouted warming up, it was deceptive. There was power and technique in that jiggling torso. Overweight, gifted, funny, and without fear, Danny had a winning record; it would have been much better if he didn't run out of gas so quickly. But, together, they'd handle him.

Whether it was his mother who had bought them — no one asked — Rob wore black velvet trunks for the McNair fight. He didn't seem the least self-conscious, though Pearce certainly noticed, and he was sure others did as well. Nothing was said, Danny didn't make a joke or point, but Pearce was silently, uncomfortably, aware of them. They seemed a bad omen. Regardless of how well muscled, the boy's legs showed so pale against the material: short, out of proportion to his body. "Those things'll be too hot," Pearce said under his breath.

"What's that?" Rob asked.

"Nothing." Fingering the cloth, Pearce wondered how heavy it would be when it got wet. "I better not spill water on you."

"Really?"

"Of course not."

Before the first round was a minute old Pearce could hear Jimmy, his voice carrying from the rear of the armoury, just where he was supposed to be: "Finish him, finish him!"

They'd hardly closed. Pearce was irritated with such foolish shouting. Robbie was punching.

Danny came on. Got stung, shook it off, came on. Robbie jammed his arms, banged them. A counter jab moved Rob's head back but didn't stop him from reaching underneath for a liver shot. He met elbows so went wide the other way, hook hook, mottling Danny's ribs and side.

Game, intent, his composure intact, shifting sideways but always moving forward, Danny advanced.

Maybe Jimmy had seen something no one else had, for Rob commenced to beat on Danny. Unanswered. Beat the protective ball of gloves, skull, and hugging forearms that curled up before him. Finish him! Rob didn't need to be told, he was trying. Pearce was taken aback. He knew, he just knew, that when Danny lashed out of that defensive crouch it would be ineffective.

Is it that I'm not needed? he wondered. I should celebrate, the kid had all a champion was supposed to have, all the clichés from thirty years in boxing: killer instinct, controlled ferocity, finish. And Pearce was shocked.

Was it something he had seen in Rob's first professional bout, a small thing he had dismissed, tried to ignore? After the TKO they'd hugged, "good fight, good fight," and like all losers the man with the eye full of blood had smiled in a different way than the winner: more gracious, or grateful. They'd both followed the form, but Pearce saw Rob as too perfunctory. All winners were, they almost had to be, but Rob seemed genuinely without feeling.

Old man, there's something wrong with you, he told himself. They aren't playing the piano up there. But then, as so often with Rob, he saw what he had not before, what he might have spent a lifetime denying. It was as if all those instructions in punching he had given over the years — drive your fist through to the back of his head — were suddenly real.

But Danny isn't hurt bad like that, Pearce thought. Red-faced, courageous, intelligently defensive, he covered up, he turtled, but he did not seem afraid. This is not the time for mercy, Pearce told himself, that can come after. Was it that Rob wouldn't feel it then?

Is this about sportsmanship, or some idea I have of it? Retire, Pearce told himself. If he had not taught the subtleties Rob was using now, always getting the last shot out of a clinch or at the bell, the gratuitous little taps to the kidneys or the back of the neck, someone else would have. Why shouldn't the lad know about them, because they can be about winning and he was certainly going to win.

There was a surge from Rob. Pearce never thought he would see the day Danny wouldn't fight back. All he could think, as he listened to the noise, was flab smackin', slab whackin'.

His head's protected, Pearce thought, but Rob'll beat him to death. My boy's magnificent. Think of how he goes easy on sparring partners, think of that. Because here he'll kill him. He could.

CHAPTER **22**

FIRED, AS HE HAD SENSED HE WOULD BE, but not before Rob was really ready for this match, Pearce paced just out of reach of the light from a refreshment stand. A shadow curtain, separating the walkway behind the last row of chairs and the harsh, spare light of the booths, began abruptly. This far away from the ring there were blocks of empty seating; the lighter weights still didn't draw. Pearce did not consider sitting down.

They were going in now, Shiner and Lucy in matching black windbreakers, Robbie's name across the backs in white silk. The boy wore a white shortie robe, trimmed in black. There was no writing on it.

He's carrying his own bucket! What kind of a goddam operation was it? Pearce trembled, wished there was someone he could phone, talk to, pray to. His old man's claw hands, which is how he thought of them, trembled like the palsy. Blue-veined, fine, thin-skinned, long-fingered hands. They should be helping. He stepped into the passageway light to examine them, anything but look at the mill and excitement of the procession to the ring.

Unable to stay away long, Pearce strode three steps back into the darkness. There was Rob climbing up. At least the ropes were held open for him.

Boy, did he look ready. Running on the spot, shaking his arms out, shadow boxing, his shimmering garment fluid and shiny under the lights, Rob seemed someone Pearce both didn't know, a product almost, and the lad he had spent so much time with. There was also that great impersonal excitement that could come with the fights: it was about to begin. The happy anxiety of the crowd — the tension was theirs as well as the fighters', yet it couldn't really touch them. The assurance and high spirits on display affected Pearce as they always did, no matter how indifferent he tried to appear, especially when he was working. Rob was special, and the crowd anticipated as if this was a championship fight, not just a preliminary.

"What do you think, partner?" Mr. Rocco also kept to the dark side of the arena's high level, and walked towards Pearce with a hot dog in one hand and a soft drink in the other. In the bad light his double-breasted pinstripped suit acted like camouflage.

"I'm not a partner any more, as you can see." Without glancing at the refreshments, Pearce felt like asking Rocco about his diet.

"That's okay." Rocco bit into the hot dog. "They fired Jimmy. You were next, what did you expect? They think they don't need anybody, they'll have it all for themselves. What do you think?" he said with his mouth full.

"He sure looks good, doesn't he?"

Rocco took another bite.

"Is it good?" Pearce asked. He couldn't help himself, half sarcastic and half really worried about rat hairs and fat and Rocco's health. I've spent too many years worrying about things like the food other people eat, Pearce thought. It's a habit I've got to break.

The other fighter was in now.

"It'll be a good fight." Rocco seemed as lively and happy as Pearce had ever seen him.

"You think Rob'll have any trouble with this guy?"

"I don't think you'll be up here long, is what I think," Rocco said.

It was what Pearce hoped, and it was what he wanted to hear; his heart lifted. "Pardon?" He wanted to hear it again.

"Come on, let's go sit down," Rocco said.

They moved down the aisle. Pearce, the taller of the two, seemed to have some difficulty. Briefly he put his hand on Rocco's shoulder, as if he was being led.

I've never thought of Rocco Canzanno as short, he thought, and he's very short. "My night vision's gone," Pearce said.

"Let's sit in here." They were close enough to see well but remained in one of the dimmest parts of the huge circle surrounding the ring, no one else near them.

◤

"Did you hear what happened to Shiner in Milton?" There, Pearce came right out and asked him.

"What's the delay down there?"

There was a problem in Robbie's corner. Shiner got down, walked a few steps back towards the dressing rooms, then turned and climbed back into the ring, shrugging as he got there.

"No water bottle," Pearce said. "It looks like they don't have one. No mouthpiece? If it's no mouthpiece there's no fight."

"No, he has a mouthpiece," Rocco said. "It's in."

"Early," Pearce said. "It's in early."

The referee waved both parties into the middle.

"They didn't bring a water bottle." Pearce shook his head. "Unbelievable."

"You take that guy too seriously," Rocco said. Between thumb and forefinger, he held the remains of his hot dog, a bulbous wad of meat. "He's nothing." He popped the tidbit into his mouth.

"Excuse me, sir," Pearce said. "He's down there and we're up here. Shiner's won, even if they need a water bottle."

"You going to run down there and find one? Siddown. I know what you're saying about Mr. Shiner," Rocco said. "But let it play. Let it play out."

"All I am is worried about the boy," Pearce said.

"That so?"

"I know you are too."

"Sure."

The bell rang.

"He's special," Pearce nearly pleaded. "He's a special talent."

"He's a nice kid," Rocco said.

◤

Whether they had a water bottle or not didn't matter, because Shiner and Lucy did so little they probably wouldn't have used one anyway.

After round one Rob returned to his corner with an anguished look on his face. He wasn't in any trouble, but he looked like he was mouthing the words, "Where's Stu?"

"Look at that," Rocco said. "They miss you already."

Leaning forward, Pearce threw a long looping uppercut.

"He can't see you," Rocco said.

Pearce did it again.

"You're supposed to be watching this," Rocco said. Though Pearce had not quite mimed the movements, the jabs and feints, of the men in the ring, he looked ready to. It irritated Rocco. "He can't hear you, either."

"I didn't say anything," Pearce said, then, indicating a very small uppercut at Rocco, "It's what he needs to do."

"Did you ever box, Mr. Pearce?"

"It seems I've been asked that before," Pearce said wearily. "And yes, I did. Not like you, or Jimmy, but I did. Never pro, though, not like you."

Was it the way he looked, throwing that punch in his loose overcoat, his woodpecker-grey hair standing up, his long face? Not knowing quite why — was it Pearce's identification with the boy, a happiness that seemed out of proportion? — Rocco tried to put a damper on the very idea of boxing. He just did. "Why would anyone want to do a thing like that, eh?"

"What, box? You did, you loved it."

"I loved it, eh?"

"You did," Pearce said. "You loved it. And you liked to spar more than train, and fight more than spar. You told me."

"You got me there," Rocco said. "I loved it. But I

got out before I got hurt. Some people say 'good fight' to guys. They don't know what's gone on."

"I've been in the game a long time," Pearce said.

"The game," Rocco said. "It isn't a game."

"I've been around boxing a long time. At the amateur level, yes. That's where I've been. And it's called the fight game."

"Okay," Rocco said.

"Well, being out of it, and I'm really out of it here, really drives it home."

"Drives what home?"

"That I miss being part of it."

"Look at him putting his mug in there." Rocco nodded at Shiner giving instructions. His face was close to Robbie's, but he didn't seem to be saying much. "You're a local guy, and you're as good as anyone. You'll be part of it."

◢

In the next two rounds Rob did try to put punches together, and he would plant and throw, but nothing much came of it. Irrepressible, Pearce nudged Rocco during the flurries. "He's like old Tom Longboat, what they said about him: now I run, now I *go*. Look at him. Look at him go."

"He's not that effective, he's not that good," Rocco said.

"Tonight."

"Okay, tonight. He's not having the best night."

"But he can do it," Pearce said.

"He's catching too many punches, from a guy like that."

"Wasn't that your specialty?" Pearce said. "You

were a tough guy from what I hear. Taking three to give one."

"Not three. Boxing's about getting hit, but he shouldn't be getting caught like he is. He looks good, he looks like he's not, but he's getting caught."

"Be patient," Pearce said.

"I'm nothing but."

◥

Alone and looking up in the parking lot, Rocco saw a great change in the weather. Though black as midnight, his big Lincoln appeared to be waiting for him; higher up a huge transformation was taking place. He and all that was around him, the buildings, the cars, what trees there were, the contours of the landscape itself, seemed insubstantial.

He paused with his keys in the door. He tried to think of the fight, which Robbie had won on a late Sunday afternoon. Shiner had proved to be more difficult to do anything about than he had ever imagined. Rocco smiled when he remembered Lucy saying, "Shine can't take a hint." The two bozos who had gone to visit him must surely have done more than hint; he would dearly love to know what they'd said.

During the match Rocco had stayed beside Pearce, but then Pearce and Jimmy had found each other, and he now saw them headed out of the arena together, leaning into the wind.

Sacrifice and the night sky.

It was not a memory from a catechism lesson, or mass; there was no awareness of the sky then. Was it about what had gone on, here below, on this land no matter how changed? And that above, moving.

Forever.

Fragments of darkness, torn across a face of cobalt blue. No, what was wider than all the world. Cold. A huge wind high up.

He was not afraid.

Winter coming on.

C H A P T E R **23**

JIMMY WAS COMING OVER, to ask about coming back, and to ask for Pearce too. Robbie waited in his room.

The vacuum cleaner was stored behind his door now. They had more than one.

There were other things in his closet, boxes and pots and cartons, two steam irons, one with enamel, one stainless steel. They were piled and falling over; they were not his.

And there was too much food these days, as if there were more than two people living in the apartment, as if Shiner was over more than he was. He saw less of Shiner now.

On the kitchen counter was half a chiffon pie — he'd had the other half after lunch for dessert. Too much.

The daydream he was in, which paralyzed and protected him, in which he visualized what else was out there, had nothing to do with eating, or feeling sick. It stopped him from being sick.

The chiffon pie was fresh from Hunt's. Beside it was part of a strawberry-rhubarb pie, a ham too big to get in the fridge, a wedge of dry, crumbling angel food cake, some cherries, and a dish made up of cream, chocolate cookies, marshmallows, custard, and other things that was called Better Than Sex. There were chicken wings, breaded liver with bacon, slices from a roast of beef — his mother always called it "a roast of beef," not roast beef. The mustard spread on the meat softened as it was cooked, it didn't harden. The best slices were the outside ones.

"Eye of the round," she used to say that, "eye of the round," but he didn't know what it looked like.

Broccoli in sauce with cheese, scalloped potatoes, stuffed olives, cashews; slices of processed ham, slices of processed cheese. Why weren't they in the fridge? There was room in the fridge for them.

Lucy had brought it all home from a party. The oil and vinegar of the tossed salad would be room temperature after sitting there all night. Did it get more watery when that happened?

A dry turkey with darkening parsley around it.

"The juice of the meat," Lucy always said, "the juice of the meat." He couldn't remember if any lay under the beef; he couldn't picture it. Blood and fat, only blood and fat.

Pineapple and maraschino cherries on the ham.

Here in his room was the bed on which he lay, with its taut maroon bedspread; a desk against the wall, a lamp with a twistable metal neck — he thought of it as one eye, an eye that overheated — and a chair. His trophies sat on the window sill. Beyond them was the yellow brick of the apartment building behind. Nine stories below, off to the side, at the backyard of one of the houses left on Spenser Avenue, were the purple-green leaves of a tree. It looked like a bush from high up. Darker than from below. A red maple. He didn't have to get up to see it.

The walls were dark pink. No pictures. The sand fine as flour that seemed to be below every window in the apartment did not touch his trophies, except at their base. She had put a bowl among them, covered with wax paper. Brush the bowl, lift it up, and you'd feel granules.

The way this always ended was he would suddenly get up and get busy, but he did not want to now.

The emptiness he felt was his own. It was all he had just then. It would end, it was only a part of his life; he would float for a moment. His heart could beat fast and it didn't matter. Part of him, not all of him, it was part of him. Robbie closed his eyes.

◢

Hesitating outside, where he must have been for over an hour, Jimmy had really not expected Shiner to pull up.

A bad move, it would be a bad move, but watching the motion of his long car jouncing into the side lot, then the smooth, assured sweep into a spot, made Jimmy decide to go in. Right then.

The apartment building had blue sheets of vinyl-facing across its front, separating each floor: windows, brick, balconies, and the blue, and a glass lobby. It was the most colourful building on the street, but didn't have a name. Others did. Jimmy wondered why it wasn't called The Mermaid or something. They weren't far from the lake. But in a city you never thought of it as a lake. What good was it?

"Hello, Mr. Maclean, Mr. Shiner," Jimmy said.

Without hostility Shiner turned a large shoulder to him and attempted to go in. He slid one hand into his coat front as he opened the door; like Napoleon, Jimmy thought, except he's goddam big. "Hold up, please, Mr. Shiner, hold up."

Shiner stopped. "What's there to say?"

He's not angry and he's not afraid, Jimmy saw, and despite himself he felt grateful that Shiner was talking to him. It made him speak the truth, not that he knew what else to do, though he thought there could have been some other plan.

"That time at the party, eh . . ."

"Yep."

"Well, that was a while ago. Look, Mr. Shiner, look. Pearce and I were at the fight the other night. And, well, it's the way he was crowdin' in there. That's not right. He's really a counter puncher, Robbie's a really good counter puncher, the guy was set up for it, but Robbie just wades in and bangs."

"He's undefeated," Shiner said.

"Yes, yes, he is," Jimmy said.

"Did Pearce have the same analysis?"

"Sure he did, a' course he did, Mr. Shiner. Stu saw the fight too."

"Did he send you here to tell me that?"

"No, no. Not at all. I mean, he knows I came. I mean, I told him I was coming."

"Uh-huh."

"Rob didn't have to lead against a hitter like that, even if he could outhit him! He was taking everything to get inside. He didn't need to do that. He took hooks he shoulda blocked. Now Stu did say that. And the other guy was countering Robbie's jab, that's not right!" With enthusiasm and conviction Jimmy rose to his subject, and not only because Shiner showed he was interested.

"Ride up to the apartment with me," Shiner said. "I think we'll talk to Lucy."

In the elevator, tall and unsmiling, making a move as if he was about to tuck his hand in the coat front again but thinking the better of it, Shiner stood beside Jimmy.

Sensing he had Shiner on his side, implying he would be an ally when they talked to Lucy, Jimmy said, "You're like a father to him, eh."

"Me?" Shiner said. "Not me."

"I mean, you know what's best. Like your own father gave you the good advice," Jimmy said. "He knew what was best. When to put things aside." He now felt ashamed of his brawl with Shiner. "I mean, the parent is the parent. Your father, he knew what was best for you."

"My father," said Shiner, "was an absence."

"Oh."

"A violent one," Shiner said: all that time we spent together, I never knew him. He saw his father in the cab of the White; he remembered the creak of his steps on the floorboards when he got home, late. Years apart. The old man might never have been there, but we weren't without him. How old would I have been? Shiner saw snare wire, copper snare wire — where'd he get that? — whipping into his legs when he was wearing short pants.

"Jeeze, eh," Jimmy said.

"We got three squares a day," Shiner said as he

always did, then added, "He wasn't bad after we were sixteen."

"I know what you mean," Jimmy said, thinking about what he would say to Lucy. Here they were, the ninth floor, the top floor.

As Jimmy stepped forward Shiner stopped him. "If you come back it's going to be a little different, how things are arranged."

"That's fine," Jimmy said. "Fine."

"We'll see," Shiner said.

"She's his mother, eh," Jimmy said when Shiner got out his keys. "I mean, she'll see."

Matter-of-fact, without any kind of resentment, Shiner said, "He's her everything. I've heard the little girl say it."

"Oh yes," Jimmy said, with appetite. "Uh-huh."

CHAPTER **24**

"BOY, THAT SOUTH PARKDALE, EH." Jimmy was wrapping his hands. "How it's changed."

"A lot of good it's done the people who live there," said Pearce.

"There's a big hole beside your building, eh, Rob. When I was down there, there was a big hole beside your apartment building."

"That's Bruce St. Clair's house," Robbie said. "A guy next door."

"It ain't a house no more."

"He joined the army," Rob said.

"The Canadian military?" asked Pearce.

Robbie nodded.

"About your age?"

"Kinda."

"That's a brave kid going away from home like that," Pearce said.

"Brave!" said Jimmy. "Is he ranked number ten in the country?"

"No, leaving home," Pearce said.

◪

They would make quite a lot of money on this fight. As they drove along the Lakeshore in the autumn night, Lucy was glad she had left her leotard on under her slacks. The lake to their left was black and cold, you could never see the end of it; there was wind. Far ahead, sticking out into the water like a dimly lit barge, she could see the Palais Pier. Although she could not see whitecaps, Lucy imagined waves booming and backing up into others in a confusion of waters around its base. It made her think of being alone on a freighter on a dark sea, an idea that should have been full of fear, but was only of loneliness.

And there would be, as she stood on the lip of the ship's steel hold, curiosity, anticipation; the voice of her mother long ago but not too far away saying, "Where is that child?" That is what she used to say when Lucy was under the porch, reading.

"We're all right for time," Shiner said to her.

She wanted to check her makeup, but with her hand on her purse decided not to.

Now Jimmy and Pearce were back handling Robbie he didn't need her as much. With the yoga class not getting out until seven o'clock it was better he go down with them.

It was not just the exercises that were healthy, for her, but what she learned about nutrition — that would be good for Rob. Shiner was indifferent to her taking the lessons and she knew he would submit to what she learned from the new books she had: about desiccated liver pills, and brewer's yeast she would make him take in orange juice, no matter how it tasted.

Smiling, Lucy pulled her clothes tight around her and pushed into the upholstered door of the big automobile. Green light from the dashboard did not quite reach her face.

◢

He'd heard about pissing blood, and he had been sore after the last fight, but it would never happen to him. The window in the washroom was high up and opaque, with thin wire running through the glass. It seemed like nothing beyond, nothing of the night, could get inside. There were cobwebs, a streak of paint.

The gauze on Robbie's hands reminded him of a mummy's bandages. He held his hands high up, away from his body, and wiggled the fingertips. Jimmy had done a good job.

Pausing before going back, Robbie stretched out his arms, doing circles, then full windmills. He didn't want to leave this quiet, still place. He bent his torso; he could move so freely. Suddenly he stood straight and snaked his arm around his neck to get at an itch on his back. He smiled at the urgency he felt; he was almost choking himself with his own forearm.

Years ago, after his father died, Lucy had what she called the itch. She'd been "driven half mad" with it — he recalled the words and the way she just had to scratch whenever it came on. There seemed nothing anyone could do; cornstarch baths hadn't helped. Now, he realized, he had wanted it to stop so much he almost wanted to scratch for her, to climb into her skin. His smile broadened. "The itch, the itch," she'd said, lips drawn back over her teeth, biting. "I got the itch."

And he laughed aloud, not at his mother, or at the old upset, but with the freedom he felt in his own shoulders; the stance he took beside these cell-like cubicles. "The itch," he said.

When he got back both Pearce and Jimmy were arguing.

"You gotta hate the guy, you gotta take that fear and use it," Jimmy said.

"I honestly don't believe that, my man, and either do you. How many of your opponents did you hate?"

"If you're nervous, I mean," Jimmy said.

"Nothing sustains like hate, eh," Pearce said. "Because almost anything is better than being afraid."

"Maybe," Jimmy said. "Sort of."

"Well, I'm telling you, you don't have to be afraid. You have to think about what you're going to do. You have to concentrate. Of course there's nerves. But if you think about what you have to do, on the practical, technical problems involved, not even that, just about what you have to do and what you can do, not great big fantasies, but what you can really, practically do, and focus on that, then all this fury stuff . . . You okay, kid?"

"I can scratch myself now." He thrust his hands towards them. "I can scratch myself all over."

"Yeah?" Jimmy said. "Well, let me get the gloves on. We'll be going down soon."

Still lighthearted, Robbie said, "I thought about pissing blood."

With a concern so serious he wondered if it sounded genuine, Pearce asked, "Has that ever happened to you, son?"

"Of course not," Robbie said.

"He ain't met any big body punchers," Jimmy chortled.

"You okay?" Pearce asked.

As he pushed a sleeve of one glove up Rob's wrist, Jimmy lifted his legs up and down, as if running on the spot, a little antic dance.

"You're a little pale," Pearce said. "We gotta get you slicked up."

"What would happen if I didn't go down?" Robbie asked casually.

"Lemme get this other one on," Jimmy said. "Your folks'll be here soon."

"Nothing would happen," Pearce said. "The sun would come up tomorrow."

"Do you mean that, Stu?"

"You don't have to go down."

"Stu's right. You should move around a little, break a sweat," Jimmy said. "Move around a little."

"Don't you want to fight?" Pearce asked with the same seriousness he had used before.

"It's not that," Robbie said.

"He has to fight," Jimmy said. "What the hell are you talking about? His folks will be here soon."

Without looking at him Pearce told Jimmy, "They won't be coming to the dressing tonight. I talked to them earlier."

"Oh."

"I don't know," Robbie said. "Maybe I don't want to."

"Oh dear Lord." Jimmy threw a towel on the floor.

"Just a minute," Pearce said. He addressed the boy. "You don't have to go on, Rob, that's the truth."

"I'm getting his parents." Jimmy left the room.

Pearce said, "You don't have to, no."